Taking a deep breath to steady her nerves, Suzy pulled the door open, braced herself and then walked in.

The smell of dust and mold assaulted her nose the second she entered. She let the door close behind her as she looked around.

"Hello? Is anyone here?" Suzy called out.

Only the echo of her own voice answered her.

Had she gotten the address wrong? Was the kidnapper jerking her around, sending her to the wrong place to show her that he was holding all the cards and that she had none?

But she *did* hold a card, Suzy silently insisted. She dug in, holding her ground and giving it one more try.

"Look, I came here just like you told me to. Now stop playing games and show yourself, damn it!" she demanded.

There was still no answer, but she couldn't shake the feeling that she was being watched. What was this creep's game?

D0042626

Dear Reader,

As you may have noticed this month, Harlequin Romantic Suspense has a brand-new look that's a fresh take on our beautiful covers. We are delighted at this transformation and hope you enjoy it, too.

There's more! Along with new covers, the stories are longer—more action, more excitement, more romance. Follow your beloved characters on their passion-filled adventures. Be sure to look for our newly packaged and longer Harlequin Romantic Suspense stories wherever you buy books.

Check out this month's adrenaline-charged reads:

COWBOY WITH A CAUSE by Carla Cassidy

A WIDOW'S GUILTY SECRET by Marie Ferrarella

DEADLY SIGHT by Cindy Dees

GUARDING THE PRINCESS by Loreth Anne White

Happy reading!

Patience Bloom

Senior Editor

MARIE FERRARELLA

A Widow's Guilty Secret

HARLEQUIN®

entertain, enrich, inspire™

If you purchased this book without a cover you should be aware that this book is stolen property. It was reported as "unsold and destroyed" to the publisher, and neither the author nor the publisher has received any payment for this "stripped book."

Special thanks and acknowledgment to Marie Ferrarella for her contribution to the Vengeance in Texas miniseries.

Recycling programs
for this product may
not exist in your area.

ISBN-13: 978-0-373-27806-0

A WIDOW'S GUILTY SECRET

Copyright © 2013 by Harlequin Books S.A.

All rights reserved. Except for use in any review, the reproduction or utilization of this work in whole or in part in any form by any electronic, mechanical or other means, now known or hereafter invented, including xerography, photocopying and recording, or in any information storage or retrieval system, is forbidden without the written permission of the publisher, Harlequin Enterprises Limited, 225 Duncan Mill Road, Don Mills, Ontario M3B 3K9, Canada.

This is a work of fiction. Names, characters, places and incidents are either the product of the author's imagination or are used fictitiously, and any resemblance to actual persons, living or dead, business establishments, events or locales is entirely coincidental.

This edition published by arrangement with Harlequin Books S.A.

For questions and comments about the quality of this book please contact us at CustomerService@Harlequin.com.

® and TM are trademarks of Harlequin Enterprises Limited or its corporate affiliates. Trademarks indicated with ® are registered in the United States Patent and Trademark Office, the Canadian Trade Marks Office and in other countries.

www.Harlequin.com

Printed in U.S.A.

Books by Marie Ferrarella

MARIE FERRARELLA

This *USA TODAY* bestselling and RITA® Award-winning author has written more than two hundred books for Harlequin Books and Silhouette Books, some under the name Marie Nicole. Her romances are beloved by fans worldwide. Visit her website, www.marieferrarella.com.

To Patience Bloom,

For constantly making this fun, not work.

Prologue

Mabel Smith knew something was wrong the moment she walked into the house.

She could *feel* it.

Feel it despite the fact that there were no signs of a struggle and nothing out of place.

The longer she stayed, the more convinced she became that she was right.

As was her custom, the petite, pleasantly plump housekeeper had let herself into Professor Melinda Grayson's modern, two-story house with her own key. It was a copy of the master key, awarded to her amid much fanfare. She viewed the key as a status symbol, a testimony to her character.

Her employer, Melinda Grayson, did not trust easily, holding the people she dealt with suspect until they proved themselves worthy in her eyes. As someone who cleaned the woman's house and perforce was given access to every corner of it, she'd been watched with an eagle eye for the better part of two years.

At the beginning of Mabel's third year of service, the renowned, somewhat controversial and eccentric sociology professor dramatically bestowed her with a copy of the house key, making Mabel literally *swear* that she would never allow anyone else even to hold it, much less use it. It was a well-known fact that Professor Grayson guarded her own privacy as zealously as she delved into everyone else's when she was doing research for one of her highly contentious books.

Entering the house that she'd cleaned from top to bottom once a week, Mabel had expected to find the professor somewhere on the premises. The woman's car, a sky-blue vintage 1957 Chevy Impala, one of her few extravagances, was parked in the driveway. Since that was her only mode of transportation to and from Darby, the college where Dr. Grayson taught, Mabel had assumed that the woman was in the house somewhere, possibly working on a paper or getting lectures ready for the new, upcoming academic year.

But when she called out her greeting, the housekeeper received no answer.

That in itself was no cause for concern. More often than not, the professor was either lost in thought or uncommunicative. However, she always made an appearance within a few minutes of Mabel's entry, just to make certain that the woman had come alone and hadn't brought someone with her to help with the work.

Not that she ever did. Dr. Grayson had made it abundantly clear that she did not care to have any uninvited strangers walking across her floors, nor would she tolerate it.

"Something is wrong," Mabel said to herself, speaking loudly enough for someone else to hear—had there *been* someone else in the room to hear, which apparently there was not.

Feeling progressively ill at ease with the situation and possessing an extremely healthy and active imagination, Mabel still forced herself to clean the house, hoping she was just being unduly concerned.

When there still appeared to be no sign of the professor, she felt she had no choice but to place a call to the local police.

Private creature or not, she knew the professor would have wanted her to call them.

He didn't hear the phone ring at first.

Didn't realize the next few minutes would upend his life.

Oil baron Gabe Dawson was in Malaysia on important business, far away from Vengeance, Texas. He finally picked up the hotel phone.

"Gabe. You need to come home. Now. It's Melinda," his assistant said.

It was only when he heard his ex's name that he froze. Gabe stopped and sat on the bed, braced for the news.

"She was kidnapped." His assistant gave him some details, but there was little information. Just that someone had made her disappear.

Along with the shock, a wave of nostalgia came over him and he allowed himself to drift back and remember. Remember how things used to be with Melinda. In the beginning. Back when they had been just two overachieving graduate students, wildly in love and bound and determined to leave their marks on the world.

Melinda had been even more focused on that than he'd been. She'd been resolute about making a name for herself—her *own* name—as if she wanted everyone she had ever known from birth to know that this was what Melinda Grayson had become. It was important to her, to the exclusion of everything else.

Eventually, even he had found himself excluded, standing on the outside of her world.

In hindsight, he supposed they began growing apart almost from the very moment they took their vows before a justice of the peace ten years ago. Melinda started pointing her finger at what she perceived were social injustices, while he, with his well-honed business acumen, became a recognized leader in his field, and exceedingly wealthy to boot.

With his bank accounts totaling in the billions, he, in effect, found himself becoming the enemy against whom Melinda was so profoundly railing.

Looking back, he accepted that their divorce was inevitable.

But in the beginning, ah, the beginning, there had been some really good times. Excellent times.

"What else can you tell me?" Gabe asked.

"It is suspected that the professor was kidnapped from her home. You're the closest to immediate family that can be located. The Dean of Darby College has put in a plea that the kidnappers get in contact with him and make their demands known."

"Get me on the next flight," Gabe said. *"I'm her family,"* he emphasized. He was aware that Melinda had siblings, but she never talked about them and he never prodded her. The estrangement, he'd gathered, went way back.

Melinda had been his first love. Though they became as different as fire and ice, he'd never loved anyone as much as he had loved her. Most likely, he never would.

If something had happened to Melinda, then he wanted to help get her back. God knew, if money was the issue, it wouldn't be for long. He had more money than he could possibly spend in a lifetime.

Two lifetimes.

Gabe started toward the winding staircase. He needed to pack.

Wouldn't it be ironic if the very money that Melinda had once turned her nose up at would come to her rescue?

He didn't know if that would come under the heading of poetic justice or not but it would certainly point to the fact that God had an incredibly sardonic sense of humor.

Chapter 1

Where *was* he?

Frustrated, Suzy Burris dropped the curtain she'd pushed back from the living room window and sighed loudly. Of all the evenings for Peter to be late getting home, he had to pick this one.

Probably seeing one of his women, she thought angrily.

And if she asked him about it, he'd look at her with that engaging smile of his and tell her he was busy with official business. "County sheriff business," he'd clarify, and then he'd tell her that he wasn't at liberty to share that "business" with her. Because she had "no need to know."

Bull.

That's all it was. Pure and simple *bull.* Like all the other times.

And she was tired of it.

Tired of the lies, tired of going through the motions and pretending that everything was all right, when it wasn't.

And it hadn't been for a long, long time.

Suzy could feel her whole body vibrating with impatience. She'd finally, *finally* made up her mind that despite the beautiful two-month-old baby boy mercifully asleep now in the nursery, her marriage to Peter was not about to recover. It had been on life support for a long time now and it was currently in its very last death throes. And while it really bothered her that she'd never loved him the way a wife was supposed to love a husband, there was nothing she could do to change the situation.

Like an epiphany, it had suddenly become crystal clear to her this morning that they, she and Peter, *both* needed to move on.

Suzy wanted a divorce and although he'd mentioned nothing along those lines himself, she was fairly convinced that her husband wanted it, too.

Why else had Peter been tomcatting around like that, turning to other women when she was right there, at home?

It had been hard for her, with her emotional state less than rock solid thanks to what having given birth had done to her hormones. But she'd had to admit to herself that there was no hope for them. No light at the end of the tunnel.

Just more tunnel.

The baby was supposed to have been that light, and his conception and subsequent birth clearly was a tactic that had misfired.

The baby had been a mistake.

Not that she didn't love Andy more than she'd ever thought humanly possible, but as far as his being the miracle that would heal and save their marriage, well, that just wasn't going to happen.

Suzy realized that she was back at the living room window, lifting the curtain and staring off into the darkness.

She wanted this to be over with, wanted it behind her.

Breaking her own rule, she'd even tried to call Peter a couple of times, to no avail. The phone had gone to voice mail immediately each time.

He had to be with a woman.

When Peter was on the job as the county's sheriff, he never shut off his phone. He'd told her that was because he never knew who might be trying to reach him. So if he *wasn't* with a woman, why was it off now?

Her frustration mounted as she continued to scan the darkness for some sign that he was finally approaching the driveway.

What was all this drama and mystery about? Or was she reading into things because her impatience insisted on steadily rising with each passing minute?

Given a choice, she wanted to avoid scenes like this morning at breakfast. Despite getting very little sleep the night before because Andy kept fussing, she'd done her best to give patching things up between Peter and her one more try this morning. She'd made Peter breakfast—waffles with eggs and sausages, his favorite—and tried to get some sort of a conversation going.

But she might as well have been trying to program a robot. The words she all but wound up pulling out of her husband had been stilted, cold, as if they were two strangers who'd just met and *hadn't* clicked, the way they had at that glitzy Dallas nightclub where she'd first met him.

She had come to socialize that night and Peter had been working private security at the club. The second their eyes met, the attraction had been instant and intense.

The trouble was, that strong physical attraction had never deepened, at least, not for her. At the time, she'd thought that it had for him, that Peter loved her. When he'd asked her to marry him, she'd accepted because she'd hoped that her own feelings would grow somewhere along the line and turn into the kind of love that was the foundation of every strong marriage.

She'd said "I do" praying that would somehow trigger the everlasting love she'd secretly always dreamed about.

She'd wanted the perfect fairy tale, happily-ever-after marriage.

But it never happened.

Although Pete seemed to love her, and he'd never laid a hand on her or physically mistreated her, Suzy knew deep down in her heart that she needed more to lay the foundations for a lasting relationship.

She also felt as if Peter was keeping things from her. Not work-related things but just *things*. He seemed to lead a secret life apart from the one he shared with her. It got to the point where she felt as if she were dealing with a photograph of a man and the actual three-dimensional man was out of reach.

On the surface, Peter was friendly, outgoing, gregarious, but after several years of marriage, she still knew very little about him. And *no* details about his childhood.

What husband keeps his past from his wife? What was it that Peter was hiding?

Or was she just being completely paranoid?

Just because you're paranoid doesn't mean that there isn't someone after you.

She supposed that she'd been hoping for some sort of last-minute breakthrough with this baby, and that was why, when Peter, completely out of the blue, had suggested having a baby, she'd agreed.

It had been an irresponsible way to go about patching up their relationship. *First* you had a stable home with two people who loved each other, and *then* you brought a baby into the equation. You didn't do it the other way around. You didn't just make a baby, and then hope everything turned out for the best.

Suzy admitted to herself that she'd been trying to create the exact opposite of what she'd grown up with: two alcoholic parents who were either drunk and passed out on any available flat or semi-flat surface, or going at one another with anything they could get their hands on when they were sober.

And whatever verbal and physical blows they threw that *didn't* land on each other, found their target in her—or her younger sister, Lori.

All she'd ever wanted was to be loved and to have someone to lean on. Someone who could be her protector if the occasion arose.

Or at least, that was what she thought she wanted when she'd married Peter. Only recently she realized she wanted more. She wanted someone to talk to. Someone who *really* talked to her as well. In essence, she wanted someone to share a life with.

That wasn't Peter.

"Come on, Peter. Come home. I need to get this over with before I lose my nerve," she pleaded.

Only the darkness heard her.

At thirty-eight, Nick Jeffries felt he'd seen it all—and for the most part, he'd left it behind him. As a former fifteen-year veteran detective on the Houston police force, he'd accepted a position on Vengeance's police force thinking that it would be a walk in the park and that chilling, stomach-turning homicides were a thing of the past. Vengeance, Texas, was one of those sleepy, picturesque little towns people dreamed about while trapped in a rat race, struggling to stay abreast of the bills, the tax man and soul-numbing, time-sapping boredom.

Apparently that wasn't the case anymore, Nick thought, looking down at the gruesome discovery made earlier that day by some enterprising geology graduate students. The students had initially been assigned to dig up and catalog several mineral specimens on the private land just on the outskirts of Darby College.

Instead, what they'd found were three male bodies buried in shallow graves and located fairly close to one another.

"Three for the price of one, huh?" Nick murmured sardonically.

The flippant comment was intended for the young man he'd been partnered with but when he looked up, he saw that the tall, baby-faced detective had done a quick about-face and was currently—and miserably—throwing up his breakfast behind the nearest tree.

"That's okay, Juarez," Nick assured the younger

man, raising his voice so that it carried. "I did the same thing when I saw my first dead body."

It actually wasn't true. For the most part, Nick Jeffries had practically been born unshakeable, but he thought it might give the young detective a measure of comfort to know that he wasn't alone or unique in his misery.

Shaking his head, Nick looked down at the three dead bodies that had been lifted from their graves.

Three separate, shallow graves—not one. Did that mean there were three separate killers, or just one with an odd reverence for the sanctity of death that had made him dig the multiple graves rather than just toss the bodies one on top of another?

And why these particular three people? Was it just convenience? The luck of the draw?

He highly doubted it.

What did these three have in common with each other, other than being buried out here just off the college campus? Did they all die at the same time, or did they meet their respective ends at different times by the same hand?

He supposed at least part of the latter question would be answered by the medical examiner after the autopsies were performed.

He wondered how long *that* would take and if

they even *had* a medical examiner around here. If not, they were going to have to find one, fast.

There were times when he really missed being in a city like Houston.

"So much for this being a sleepy little college town," Nick said, talking to Juarez as if the man had rejoined him instead of still heaving up his by now meager stomach contents behind a tree. "And let me tell you, if you thought that the media seemed frenzied and out of control when they converged here, asking questions about that Grayson woman's kidnapping, wait'll you see what happens when they get wind of this triple homicide," he predicted.

With a handkerchief held close to his mouth in case he wasn't quite finished throwing up what was left of his insides, Jason Juarez, his eyes watering, made his way back to his partner.

When he looked at Nick, his eyes appeared to be bloodshot, definitely the worse for wear.

Nick was tempted to tell him to go home, but that wouldn't solve anything. The kid needed to tough it out, Nick thought. Still, he couldn't help feeling sorry for him.

"You think that this is a triple homicide?" Juarez asked him.

It was obvious that the young detective was deliberately avoiding looking down at the uncovered bodies, which had already been on their way to becoming lunch a la carte for all the local rodents, wild animals and insects in the area.

Had he *ever* been this naive? Nick wondered. Somehow, he didn't think so.

"Well, there are three bodies buried pretty close to one another," he said to Juarez, doing his best not to let his impatience show, "and they're definitely dead, so, logically speaking, I'd say yes, there's a pretty good possibility that we're looking at a triple homicide. But if you're asking me if I think that the same person killed all three victims, that's something we're going to have to find—"

Nick abruptly stopped talking and he suddenly squatted down beside the body that was nearest to him. With an unreadable expression on his face, he gave the body a very slow once-over.

The face was not so destroyed that it prevented him from making an identification. "Correct me if I'm wrong, but isn't this the county sheriff, Peter Burris?" If that were the case, then this just took on a whole new spectrum of ramifications.

Juarez paled slightly beneath his peaked complexion. "Are you asking me to look closer?" he asked warily.

Nick rolled his eyes. "That might be helpful, yeah," he retorted.

One of the uniformed policemen, older by a couple of decades than the queasy detective, took pity on Juarez—who looked as if he wanted to bolt for the trees again—and made his way over to the body in question.

Looking at what was left of the man on the ground, the officer nodded, confirming Nick's query.

"It's the sheriff all right." Somewhat intrigued rather than repulsed, the policeman squinted and took a closer look at the other two bodies that had been unearthed at the same time. Genuine surprise registered on his leathery face. "And that looks like Senator Merris. Saw him at a fund-raiser once. I was part of the security detail." His own words seemed to hit him and he appeared properly stunned. "Holy cow, this is a real live senator."

"Not quite," Nick pointed out.

"Yeah," the policeman agreed. "There's that." He looked up at Nick, the magnitude of the situation finally hitting him. "This is big."

Rather than comment on what seemed to be

very obvious—and since Juarez was still struggling even to *glance* down, Nick directed the officer's attention to the third body. "You know him?"

The older man shuffled closer and looked at the last dead man intently for several seconds. He frowned, frustrated.

"He seems familiar, but—" he shook his head helplessly. "Sorry, can't place him."

Striking out, Nick looked pointedly at Juarez. "How about you?"

Unable to get around his duty any longer, Juarez was forced to take a look. Actually, it was more like taking a fleeting glance in the body's direction. Exhaling the breath he'd been holding, Juarez shook his dark head adamantly.

"No, I don't know him," he confirmed with relief.

But the policeman wasn't through as he continued to study the only unidentified man. Circling the body, he looked at the face from every angle.

Finally, he said, "I think he used to live around here before he went off to California—or maybe it was some other place out West." He glanced up at Nick. "He had family here if it's the guy I'm thinking of. I can ask around," he offered.

"You do that," Nick turned the offer into an instruction.

Then he turned to his boy partner. Juarez's face still lacked color. He made up his mind that come tomorrow, if things didn't change, he was working this case solo. Juarez's wife was due soon with their first child. Maybe the younger detective could take some time off and be of some use to her.

But that still left today. "You up to doing a little traveling?" he asked.

Rather than immediately answering, Juarez asked uneasily, "To where?"

"I think we need to inform the sheriff's wife that she just became his widow."

In his experience, approximately 50 percent of the men and women who were killed died at the hands of their spouse. Whether this was the case in Burris's murder remained to be seen. The sooner he ruled out the sheriff's other half, the sooner he could move on and maybe even find out exactly who was responsible for this modern-day bloodbath in a sleepy town.

He scanned what might or might not have been the actual crime scene. Things would never be the same.

Not for a lot of people.

* * *

"Did you forget your key?" Suzy called out as she yanked open the front door in response to the ringing doorbell.

It wouldn't have been the first time that Peter had forgotten his house key. But if everything went right, it would be one of the last, she thought.

Suzy did her best to contain the nervous anticipation that all but vibrated through her. She'd been up for most of the night, not because of the baby, but because she kept hearing Peter come through the door.

Each and every time it just turned out to be her imagination, hard at work. What that meant, she decided, was that she *really* wanted to get this divorce matter out and on its way.

Throwing open the front door, she found herself on the receiving end of a surprise. And not the pleasant kind, she couldn't help thinking.

Suzy instinctively took a step back.

Her hand on the doorknob, she started to close the door again, intent on locking out the strangers on her doorstep.

The sheriff's wife was quick, but Nick was quicker. He blocked her motion with his hand, at the same time putting his foot over the sill to keep the door from closing.

"We need to talk with you, Mrs. Burris," Nick said as his tongue-tied partner appeared somewhat startled by her behavior and all too ready to retreat.

Nick watched as suspicion came and then went from the pretty blonde's cornflower-blue eyes. She appeared to regard them both in silence for a moment, then said in a hushed tone, "You know my name. Why is it you know my name?"

She had a bad feeling about this—and it was escalating by the moment as she waited for an answer. She looked from one man to the other, then back at the older detective. Waiting.

"Would you mind if we stepped inside, Mrs. Burris?" Nick suggested, gesturing into her house. He was surprised when she remained planted before him. "This isn't the kind of thing a person likes to hear while standing in the doorway of her house."

Suzy raised her chin, thinking herself already prepared for the worst. "Sitting on the sofa isn't going to change whatever it is that you have to say to me, Detective…" She deliberately let her voice trail off, waiting for the tall, strikingly handsome dark-haired man to fill in the blank.

"Jeffries," he told her, then nodded toward Juarez. "And this is Detective Juarez," he added before going back to what she'd said. "No, it won't," Nick readily agreed. "But it just might help you to cushion the shock—no pun intended," he interjected when his own words played themselves back in his head. He didn't want her to think he was being flip at her expense.

Cushion the shock. Just how great a shock, she wondered. Suzy felt oddly numb, yet still somehow in control. Or so she told herself.

"Is he hurt?" she asked in a voice so quiet, it was almost a whisper. "Is my husband hurt?" she amended when neither man standing on her doorstep answered her.

"It's worse than that, ma'am," Nick told her, trying to be as gentle as possible.

Suzy felt her stomach lurch, then turn over. She struggled to pull herself together. She could handle this, she told herself. Whatever the somber-looking detective in the dark suit had to tell her, she could handle it. She could handle anything. She *had* to. She had practically a newborn depending on her. She had to remember that.

"May I see some identification, please?" she requested, holding whatever the older detective was about to say to her at bay.

Juarez fumbled for his wallet, searching his pockets, while Nick took his out and flipped it open to display his badge and ID.

Suzy could feel panic well up inside her. She barely glanced at the man's wallet, but his image registered.

"Worse than hurt," she heard herself repeating as she raised her eyes to the man's face. That could only mean one thing. Her lips felt frozen as she asked, "Is my husband dead, Detective Jeffries?"

Nick felt a wave of pity stirring. "I'm sorry to have to tell you that, Mrs. Burris, but yes, I'm afraid he is."

Every inch of skin on her body alternated between extreme heat and extreme cold.

Dead.

Peter's dead.

She waited for the wave of sorrow, of devastation to hit. But it didn't. In its place, instead, was guilt. Guilt that she didn't feel grief over his death, other than the kind of grief she might have experienced after hearing of a neighbor's death.

What kind of a person *was* she? Suzy silently demanded.

"You were right," Suzy said to the older detective, her voice sounding rather tinny to her ears as the words seemed to echo in her head.

"Right about what?" Nick asked, puzzled as he looked at her.

It was getting hard for her to breathe. "About this being easier to take on a sofa."

It was the last thing Suzy remembered saying before the bright, sunny world filtering in through her doorway went completely black.

Chapter 2

Nick prided himself on the fact that his reflexes had always been quick. This time was no exception.

One minute he was talking to the unfortunate, freshly minted widow. The next he was stretching out to catch her and keep her head—as well as the rest of her—from hitting the floor.

Beside him, Juarez stood frozen, almost in as much shock, in his own way, as the sheriff's widow. His partner was definitely in need of a crash course that would teach him exactly how to be a useful member of the police force. Right now, the man was undoubtedly well meaning, but also rather useless. The man had a great deal to learn before he could be considered a good detective.

Nick was fairly convinced that Jason Juarez had found himself in his present position only because he was related to someone either on the force, or someone who was embedded within Vengeance's less-than-dynamic town counsel. Whichever it was, the so-called guardian angel might be trying to be kind to the young man, but in the interim, he or she was setting the course of detective work back by half a century.

Juarez, he knew, was relieved when the FBI special agents had descended on the town and, specifically, the "dig" where the bodies had been found. They'd been summoned by the town fathers because one of the victims was Senator Merris. The special agents had been set to take over the entire crime scene, but he had managed to get them to agree that this would be worked as a team effort. That meant that information would be shared—supposedly.

Nick turned his attention to the woman he'd just caught. When he'd made his initial assessment of her, he'd judged that she weighed under a hundred pounds. If he wasn't right on target, he was close. Suzy Burris felt as if she weighed next to nothing at all.

Striding into the house ahead of the flustered Juarez, his arms full of unconscious damsel in distress, Nick headed straight for the sofa.

"Get the door, Juarez," he tossed over his shoulder at his partner.

It took the detective a second to process the order, and another second for embarrassment to creep up his lanky torso, reaching his cheeks and turning them a faint shade of pink.

"You want it closed?" he asked.

"No, I want you to take it off the hinges and take it with us when we leave," Nick bit off sarcastically as he lay the woman down on the sofa. "Yeah, I want it closed," he snapped quickly before the befuddled, wet-behind-the-ears detective took him at his word and started removing the door from its hinges. He wouldn't have put it past him.

The door shut and then he heard Juarez hurrying over to the sofa.

"Is she—is she all right?" the younger man asked nervously. He shifted slightly from foot to foot as he hovered about like a confused hummingbird, searching for a destination where he could alight.

"She just found out that her husband's dead, what do you think?" Nick asked, trying not to let his irritation break through. Part of that irritation had to do with the fact that he had yet to tell the woman the worst part: that her husband had been murdered.

No doubt feeling foolish, Juarez looked down at the unconscious woman. "I guess she's not all right."

There was sympathy in the younger man's voice.

At least he had the right emotional response, Nick thought. That was a start, although being *too* sympathetic wasn't a good thing, either. Nick was convinced of that. It wasn't exactly recommended for someone in their line of work. Getting too involved could get in the way, clouding their judgment and hindering them from doing their job right.

At least, that had been the case back in Houston.

Out here, when he'd accepted the job, he'd just assumed that police work involved tracking down lost dogs and occasionally finding a child who had wandered off from his or her parents. Solving homicides like the ones they were faced with came as a complete and utter surprise to him. While it was, sadly, right up his alley, Nick had come to Vengeance to take an extended break from that sort of thing.

Still, he had to admit that part of him felt suddenly alive again. He hadn't missed the nonstop pressure of the life he'd led as a detective in Houston, but he did find that he missed the challenges that sort of life had perpetually thrown at him.

At least occasionally.

"Make yourself useful," he instructed Juarez. "Get me a compress for her head."

The younger detective looked a little lost as he glanced about the room, as if searching for something to use to make this happen.

Nick sighed. This partnership was going to test his patience. If Juarez got in the way, the feds were going to want them both off the case—and as far as he was concerned, Vengeance was now his town and that made the murdered men *his* case.

"Kitchen, towel." Nick snapped out the words in staccato fashion, firing them at Juarez as if they were bullets. "Make it wet. *Cold* water," he emphasized as Juarez headed toward the section of the house where he assumed the kitchen was located. "Don't forget to wring it out," Nick added, raising his voice so that the other man could hear him.

Otherwise, Juarez would probably be bringing him a towel that left a trail of dripping water in its wake.

A beat later, Juarez cheerfully called back, "Got it!"

Nick shook his head, mentally telling himself to be patient.

When he glanced back down at the sheriff's widow, her eyes were open and she looked up at him, appearing somewhat dazed.

"Welcome back," he said, then placed his hands on her shoulders in gentle restraint as Suzy tried to sit up. "I'd hold off on that for a couple of minutes or so if I were you," he counseled, then added with a marginally amused smile, "Remember what happened the last time you ignored my advice."

Suzy sighed and remained where she was, even though it made her tense to lie down in a stranger's presence. For a second, she closed her eyes again, trying to regain her bearings.

"This isn't some cruel joke, is it?"

He heard the hopeful note in her voice and caught himself feeling sorry for her. The next moment, he banked down that emotion. He knew from experience that that was only asking for trouble.

"I'm afraid not."

She opened her eyes to look up at the man who had unwittingly thrown her world into such turmoil. "Peter's really dead?"

"He's really dead," Nick confirmed. "His body was found in a shallow grave by a group of geology grad students." After that, all hell had broken loose. It was going to be hard keeping a lid on the investigation, what with the news media already poking around.

Suzy was having trouble thinking, trouble processing this. She'd been so focused on telling Peter she wanted a divorce that this had completely thrown her for a loop.

And unleashed a great deal of guilt.

"How did he die? Was it a car accident?" she asked hoarsely.

"No." His voice was emotionless, giving nothing away. "The sheriff appeared to have been choked to death."

Her eyes widened in astonishment. "Someone *killed* him?"

Nick nodded, thinking that, all things considered, she was handling this rather well. "It certainly looks that way."

"Who?" she whispered, hardly able to force the word out.

"That's what we're currently trying to find out," Nick told her honestly.

Out of the corner of his eye, he saw the other detective approaching. Contrary to instructions, Juarez had brought back a dripping towel. He held it out to Nick like a peace offering.

Nick made no attempt to take it from him. "Mrs. Burris is conscious again, Juarez. We won't be needing that now." Then, because the detective appeared to be at loose ends as to what to do with the now unnecessary towel, Nick ordered, "Take the towel back to the kitchen, Juarez."

Happy to be given instructions to follow, the younger man quickly retraced his steps and eagerly did as he was told.

"You're very patient with him," Suzy observed.

It struck her as odd, even as she said the words, that she would notice something so insignificant, given what she'd just been told. Was she going crazy? Or was she just being insensitive to Peter's fate? Neither answer seemed like the right one.

Nick shrugged off the comment and the implied compliment behind it. "He reminds me of my kid brother," he told her. He hadn't realized that until just now, he thought, but now that he'd said it out loud, he realized that Juarez and Eddie had the same lost puppy appeal, the same eagerness to please.

It took him a second to realize that the sheriff's widow was asking him something.

"Excuse me?"

"I said, can I sit up now?" she repeated. She didn't feel up to being restrained again. She wasn't even certain just how she'd react to that.

Right now, all sorts of emotions collided within her as disbelief, anger, guilt and a sliver of relief all vied for practically the same space.

The last reaction made her ashamed. Peter had been, after all, her husband and the father of her child, relief over his death, even the barest hint of it, shouldn't be entering into the equation, she upbraided herself.

Even worse was what was missing.

What she realized was conspicuously missing was grief. *Where is the grief?* she silently demanded. Shouldn't she be feeling that predominately instead of all these other emotions that were racing through her?

What was *wrong* with her?

"Slowly," the detective was saying to her.

She blinked, confused. Had she missed something? "What?"

"You can sit up," Nick repeated. "But do it slowly," he cautioned. "You *really* don't want to get dizzy and pass out again."

She didn't like the frailty his warning implied. It wasn't as if she was made out of spun glass. If she had been, she would have shattered long before now.

"That was the first time I ever passed out," Suzy informed him with a touch of annoyance in her voice.

"First time you had a husband who was murdered, I suspect," Nick speculated.

Suzy flushed. She could feel the color rising to her cheeks, making them hot.

"Yes," she answered hoarsely, waiting to see where he was going with this.

"Drastic news brings out drastic results," he told her matter-of-factly. "Want some water?" Without waiting for an answer, he glanced at Juarez. His partner was just coming back into the room. "Juarez, get Mrs. Burris a glass of water."

Without a word, the other detective turned on his heel and went back to the kitchen.

"Makes him feel useful," Nick said in response

to the protest he saw hovering on the widow's perfectly formed lips.

"You always anticipate everything?" she couldn't help asking.

He flashed her another amused smile. Amid the vulnerability, he detected a feisty streak. He found it rather appealing.

"Saves time," he told her. "But no, I don't always anticipate everything, just the obvious things."

"Like my fainting," she assumed.

"Being told that a spouse was murdered usually comes as a shock to the person doing the listening," he said, never taking his eyes off hers.

Suzy heard the detective's emphasis on the telltale word: *usually.* Did that mean he thought that she was innocent, or did he actually think she had something to do with Peter's murder? If the latter, she knew she should be outraged at the very idea, but she still felt too drained, too devastated by the news, to summon that sort of a response.

"It did," she told him as firmly as she could, the look in her eyes challenging him to say something different.

Juarez had returned with a tall glass filled to the very brim with water. Nick put his hand out for it, then offered it to the widow.

Suzy took the glass with both hands to hold it steady and drank deeply. Strange as it seemed, the cold water helped her pull herself together and focus.

She couldn't allow herself to go to pieces. There was no one around to help her put those pieces back together again. No one to really rely on, except herself.

Just like the old days.

"Thank you," she said to Juarez, offering him the near-empty glass. Her words elicited a shy smile from the young detective as he took the glass from her.

"My pleasure, ma'am."

Ma'am. She was way too young to be a *ma'am.* Or maybe she wasn't. After all, she was someone's mother now.

"You up to some questions?" the other detective asked her. She nodded, wanting to get this over with. "When did you last see your husband?"

"Yesterday morning at breakfast." That seemed like a hundred years ago now, she thought. Had it only been a mere twenty-four hours?

"Did he seem particularly preoccupied or troubled to you?" the detective asked.

She looked at this stranger for a long moment,

wondering how to answer his question. Did she tell him that she and Peter had grown apart? That they hardly spoke to one another these last few days, except to talk about the baby? Or did she keep her secret and pretend that everything had been just fine?

Pressing her lips together, Suzy paused for a moment as she searched for some plausible middle ground. "If you're asking me if he seemed different than usual yesterday, the answer is no, he didn't."

Her words, Nick noted, were carefully orchestrated. He read between the lines.

"How long have you and your husband been having marital problems?" he asked gently.

The question surprised not only Suzy, but the other detective as well. Juarez stared at him, open-mouthed. "You didn't tell me you knew the sheriff and his wife, Nick," Juarez said, sounding slightly irritated at being shut out this way.

"I don't, do I, Mrs. Burris?" Nick asked, looking at the woman.

She didn't bother addressing his last question as she focused on the one that not only caught her off guard, but upset her, as well. She didn't want any dirty laundry to mar Peter's memory. As far as the people in the county were concerned, he was an exemplary sheriff.

"What makes you think we were having problems?" she asked.

The question told him all he asked. He was right. Had there been no problems, she might have issued an indignant denial, or at the very least, stared at him as if he was being boorish. But she didn't. She was defensive. Because there was something to be defensive about.

"Let's just say I've been there," he answered evasively.

This wasn't about him, and Nick had no intentions of revisiting his own failed attempt at marital bliss. He'd married far too young and it had all fallen apart on them not that long after the vows. In keeping with his marriage, he'd been divorced young as well. He'd learned a lesson along the way: He was no good at marriage.

"Were you two talking?" he asked, trying to sound as kind as he could under the circumstances.

"Yes," she snapped back, then shrugged helplessly as she amended, "But just barely." She paused again, searching for a way to phrase what she wanted to say. "We've just had a baby—"

"Congratulations," Juarez said with enthusiasm. "Me, too. I mean, my wife, too—except not yet. I mean—"

"He means his wife's due anytime now," Nick interjected. He'd heard about nothing else this entire last week. "Go on," he coaxed Suzy, "you were saying…?" He trailed off, waiting for her to fill in the blanks.

"Despite that, Peter's been rather distant lately," she admitted.

The next moment, she regretted the words. Why was she baring her soul to these men? What did any of this have to do with whoever had killed Peter?

"Some men feel threatened by a baby," Nick told her, recalling what he'd once heard. "They think that they're being replaced in their wives' affections."

Suzy shook her head. She wanted to stop any further conjecture before it got too out of hand.

"Having the baby was Peter's idea," she told him, then added, "he thought that the baby would bring us closer together."

He noticed she didn't say "again," which meant that they probably hadn't been all that close to begin with. Nick decided to press a little further. "How bad did it get?"

Enough was enough. Suzy's own protective instincts, the same one that had her protecting her sister from their parents' inebriated wrath, kicked in.

She glared at this intruding detective. "What does any of this have to do with my husband's murder?" she demanded.

"Just trying to establish the sheriff's frame of mind the last few days before he was killed," he replied matter-of-factly.

She really didn't like exposing her private life like this to strangers, but then, what did it matter, anyway? Peter was dead and that meant her world would have to go through some pretty drastic changes—even faster than she'd initially anticipated. After all, she *had* been planning to divorce Peter. All in all, a divorce was rather a drastic life change in itself.

She blew out a breath and plunged in. "I was going to ask Peter for a divorce when he got home last night." She addressed her words to her shoes, not feeling up to making eye contact with the detective who was doing all the questioning right about now.

But then, he'd probably take that as some sort of a silent admission of guilt, she realized. Blowing out another breath, she forced herself to look up at the man.

"Except that he didn't," she said quietly once she'd reestablished eye contact.

Something sharp pricked at his insides the moment their eyes met. Nick tried to shrug it off. It didn't budge.

"I see," he said without a shred of emotion evident in his voice, successfully masking his feelings.

It was at that moment that Detective Nick Jeffries made a stunning and rather uncomfortable discovery. He realized that he was attracted to this woman, *deeply* attracted. Moreover, it wasn't just her delicate looks that had hooked and reeled him in, it was her underlying vulnerability, which he could see she tried to cover up at all costs.

But the very existence of that vulnerability had awakened his dormant protective streak, a streak he had thought he'd successfully laid to rest more than a few years ago.

Apparently, he'd thought wrong.

Chapter 3

As Nick tried to bury this unsettling and somewhat annoying realization, Juarez's cellphone rang.

Juarez snapped to attention and seemed to go on high alert even *before* he pulled his phone out of his pocket. He blinked, clearing his vision, and then looked at the screen to identify the caller.

Rather than just answer it, the young detective continued to stare at the name, as if he couldn't believe what he was seeing.

Finally, he glanced up at Nick and said numbly, "It's my wife." The next moment, he shivered as a sudden attack of nerves seized him. His mouth choked out, "This could be it."

"It?" Nick repeated. Completely focused on the sheriff's widow, he had no idea what his partner was talking about.

Juarez nodded, still staring at the phone. "The baby's due anytime now," he said, repeating what he'd said earlier—and the day before, and the day before that. "She could be calling to tell me that she's in labor." His voice took on a panicked note as it went up two octaves, then cracked.

"Don't you think you should answer it, then?" Nick coaxed, utterly mystified at the way his partner's mind seemed to work—*if* indeed it actually *was* working at all, which he was beginning to doubt.

"Yeah, right," Juarez cried.

He fumbled with the cellphone, managing to almost disconnect himself from the incoming call before he finally hit the right key to answer it.

Juarez's hands visibly shook as he put the cellphone to his ear. "Tina? Is it time?" His eyes grew huge as he listened to his wife's answer. Literally stunned, his eyes shifted over to look at Nick. "It's time," he announced breathlessly.

He gave every indication that he was about to hyperventilate.

"Then I suggest you start breathing evenly, get in your car and go," Nick responded, uttering each word slowly, as if he were speaking to someone who was mentally challenged.

"Right. Go." As if someone had fired a starter pistol, Juarez scrambled for the door. But when he reached it, he suddenly came to a skidding stop. The rest of his brain—the part that knew it was on duty—kicked in. "What about you?" the younger detective asked. "If I take the car, you'll be stranded. How are you going to get back to the squad room?"

Nick waved away his concern. "Don't worry about me. I'll call someone," he told the other man, his tone confident. And then he ordered, "Go. Your wife needs you. And try not to hit anything on your way there," he called after the swiftly departing detective.

"Okay," Juarez yelled back.

When Nick looked back at the sheriff's widow, she had an odd expression on her face. He couldn't begin to interpret it.

"Something wrong?" he asked her.

Suzy shook her head. "I just envy his wife,

that's all," she said wistfully. "He looked really excited about becoming a father."

"He looked really clueless," Nick corrected. "And so far, that seems to be pretty much his natural state," he added in what turned out to be a completely unguarded moment. It was out of character for him. As a rule, he didn't usually let on what he thought of the people he worked with—or the ones he questioned for that matter.

"Still, he loves her." And love had a way of making up for a host of failings, she thought. "You can see it in his eyes."

Nick took his cue from her wording, following it through. "And what did you see when you looked into your husband's eyes?" he asked, curious as to what her answer would be.

Suzy shrugged in a careless manner that seemed a little too precise to him—and possibly practiced. "Barriers. Walls. Someone I didn't know."

And that, she knew, had been the true reason for the death of their marriage. Because she'd realized that after all this time, Peter was more of a stranger to her now than he had been when they'd first gotten married.

Was the woman saying that because it was how she'd actually felt, or was she laying the groundwork to distance herself from whatever the investigation would turn up about the sheriff?

She wasn't as easy to read as he'd first thought. Nick felt himself being reeled in a little further, despite his resistance to the idea. He knew he was on slippery footing.

"Did your husband have any enemies?" Nick asked her.

Suzy thought for a moment, but it really didn't matter how long she took, she decided. She would arrive at the same conclusion: she didn't think so, but she didn't know for sure.

With a sigh, Suzy shook her head. "Not that he ever mentioned, but to be honest, I really don't know. I know that Peter was away at night more and more. When I asked him about it a couple of times, he said that he was working late on a case." It had sounded like an excuse to her at the time, but maybe she was doing Peter a disservice. "Maybe he was," she said out loud. "But at the time, I thought that there was another woman in the picture—or six."

How had she arrived at that number, Nick wondered. Most women would have said one or two. "Six?"

When he said the number, it sounded foolish.

Suzy shrugged. "Sorry, that was flippant. I really don't know how many he was seeing—or *if* he actually was seeing someone else. My pregnancy had me pretty miserable and looking back, maybe I took it out on him."

Added to that, she'd worked until a little more than a week before she delivered. What that translated to, Suzy thought, was that she and Peter hardly saw each other toward the end.

Nick wasn't quite ready to allow this line of questioning to drop just yet. "Did you ever find anything concrete to back up these suspicions, something that might have got you thinking he was seeing someone else?"

"I didn't look," she admitted, unconsciously raising her chin again defensively. "I didn't want to be one of those snooping, bitter women." Besides, she thought, as long as she didn't find anything, there was always the hope that she was wrong. Other times, she was fairly sure she *wasn't* wrong. "To be honest," she continued in a distant, quiet voice, "I was a little relieved when I thought that Peter was seeing someone else."

Nick came to his own conclusions: a guilty conscience might welcome a level playing field.

"Because you were seeing someone, as well?" he guessed, watching her face intently.

Stunned, she stared at him. Despite the growing chasm between Peter and her, she'd never once thought of seeking solace in someone else's arms. She might not have been in love with Peter, but she was definitely loyal to the institution of marriage.

"What?" she cried, thinking she'd heard wrong. But the expression on the detective's face told her that she hadn't. "No, of course not. Why would you say something like that?" she asked.

"Just a natural assumption," he answered mildly. "If your husband was seeing someone, that made you feel less guilty about you seeing someone."

"You have it all wrong," she informed him with more than a touch of indignation.

"Then enlighten me."

Suzy took a breath. She really didn't like baring her soul this way, but she knew she had no choice. If she kept things back from this man, she was certain that he would think the worst.

"If Peter *was* seeing someone else, that would have made me feel less guilty about not having feelings for him."

Now, there was a novel approach to marital

discord, Nick couldn't help thinking. "I see. And when did you stop having feelings for him?"

Suzy shrugged again, her slender shoulders rising and falling beneath the light blue cotton blouse she had on. She thought of telling the detective that was none of his business, but he'd probably counter that protest by telling her that right now it was. She might as well avoid a verbal squabble with him and just answer the question.

"I don't think I ever started to have feelings for Peter, not the deep, everlasting kind. Don't get me wrong," she cautioned quickly, not wanting the detective to come away with the wrong impression. "There was a really intense attraction between us from the very first moment we met, but there turned out to be nothing behind it, nothing substantial. At least, not for me," she told him sadly. With all her heart she wished that there could have been. But this was a case where wishing just didn't make it so.

"But there was for him?" Nick questioned, watching her closely.

To him, half of police work was getting a feeling for the person you were dealing with, looking beneath their layers, their complexities. He was fairly certain that he would be able to tell if this woman was lying to him.

The answer to the last question was yes, but how did she get that across without sounding conceited?

"Well, Peter *said* he loved me, that he wanted to take care of me for the rest of my life," Suzy said. A rueful smile curved her mouth as she remembered the first stages of their relationship, before the wedding ring, the disappointments and the baby. "You have no idea how good that sounded to me at the time."

She raised her eyes to Nick and he saw a defensiveness entering the bright blue orbs, as if the woman *dared* him to find fault in her words.

"I had less than an ideal childhood," Suzy added by way of an explanation, "and just wanted someone to care whether I lived or died. Peter said he did." At the time, that seemed to be enough of a basis for marriage. "So I married him, hoping that I'd eventually feel the same way about him."

"But you didn't." It wasn't really a guess at this point but a conclusion drawn from what she'd already told him.

"Well, I didn't want him dead." And then she relented slightly, adding, "But I didn't particularly want him living with me. Especially when he was growing so distant—not that I really blamed him for that." This was all coming out really badly. To her ear, it sounded as if she was digging herself into a hole. "I began to think that the whole thing—marrying Peter—was a mistake.

"The baby wasn't a mistake," Suzy quickly added in the next breath, anticipating what the detective was probably thinking. "But on the other hand, no baby should be used as a way to keep a marriage together. It's not fair to the baby or to the two people involved."

That all sounded very noble. Maybe *too* noble, Nick thought. "Do you know how much insurance your husband was carrying?"

Suzy frowned, confused for a moment. "Life insurance?"

"Yes, life insurance," he repeated, a trace of impatience in his voice. "How much was your husband carrying?"

She was still reeling from news of Peter's murder. Practical questions like the one the detective had just posed hadn't even occurred to her yet.

"I have no idea," she told him. "As far as I know, he wasn't carrying any." And then, although she didn't want to believe anyone would even remotely think this horrible way about her, that she would kill someone, especially her husband, for money, Suzy demanded, "Why? Do you think I had him killed so I could get the insurance money?"

The whole thing was too ludicrous to believe—yet the detective obviously saw it as a possibility. Suzy didn't know whether to be angry—or afraid. Was she going to need a lawyer on top of everything else?

Nick deliberately didn't answer her directly. "It's been known to happen."

"Well, not as far as I'm concerned," she retorted angrily. Stress and overworked hormones had her fairly shouting at him. "I'm an accountant. I have a good job and I don't need extra money from some stupid life insurance policy."

"Everyone needs extra money," Nick told her matter-of-factly. And women had killed their husbands for reasons other than money.

Her eyes flashed. Okay, she was getting really tired of this verbal sparring match. If he thought she'd killed Peter for the money, she wanted him to come out and just *say* it.

"Are you trying to accuse me of something, Detective?"

Just then, before he could respond, they heard

the baby begin to cry, Andy's wails clearly audible over the baby monitor she'd placed on the coffee table. There were two more monitors scattered throughout the first floor, one in the kitchen, one in the bedroom.

But Suzy remained where she was. Waiting for an answer.

"No," Nick told her, "I'm trying to rule you *out* of something, Mrs. Burris. Where were you yesterday?"

She walked away from him and went up to the nursery. Her son needed her. "Here. At home."

Nick was right behind her, following the woman up the stairs. Walking behind her was eventful, he caught himself thinking as he watched the gentle, rhythmic sway of her hips as she went up the stairs.

"Can someone verify that?"

Stopping at the landing, Suzy looked back at him, a cynical expression on her face. It was her mask, allowing her to hide from certain people.

"The baby," she answered flatly.

He laughed shortly. The kid was a bit too young to take on the role of witness. "Can anyone older verify that?"

She thought for a moment as she went into the baby's room. It was everything that her own room—hers and her sister Lori's—was not. The space was cheerfully decorated in bright yellows and greens since she'd opted not to know the baby's gender until after he was born. It proclaimed to the world that a child was happy here—also not like her childhood bedroom.

The second she entered the nursery, Suzy did her best to shift gears. She smiled brightly at the fussing baby in the crib. At two months old, Andy was the picture of perpetual motion, his little arms and legs all going at once.

"Hi, little man. Miss me?" she murmured.

Picking up the baby, Suzy turned to look back at the detective. She expected him to be out in the hallway and was surprised to see that he had followed her into the room.

Just what did he expect to find in her son's room?

"The mailman saw me," she finally told him. "He came early and I had a bill I wanted to mail, so I hurried out before he pulled away."

That helped, but a mailman could easily be dissuaded from remembering certain facts, especially if a class act like Suzy Burris was doing the "dissuading."

"Anyone else?" Nick asked.

Suzy resented this, resented all the questions, even though she knew that it was necessary and, most likely, routine.

"My sister called me at around four o'clock yesterday to see how I was doing. Does that count?"

He nodded, couching his words carefully. "If it checks out on your phone bill, it does."

"Not a very trusting soul, are you?" she tossed over her shoulder.

From the ripe smell that was coming from Andy's lower half, she knew that the first order of business was to change him. She took him over to the changing table. Both ends of the table were buffered with the latest, most absorbent diapers on the market. Never having so much as *looked* at a diaper until two months ago, she'd gotten very proficient at changing them in the past eight weeks.

"It's not a very trusting line of business," Nick answered. "You should know that," he added, "seeing as how your husband was the county sheriff."

Was. Not *is.* It was really hard to absorb that, she thought.

"Like I said," Suzy said out loud with emphasis, "I wasn't privy to my husband's professional life. Or his private one, it's beginning to seem," she added under her breath. She spared Nick another glance as she deftly went about the task of getting rid of the soiled diaper and putting a brand-new one on the baby. "And as far as alibis go—that's what this is about, right?—*this* is my alibi," she informed him, nodding at the baby on the changing table. "Andy kept me busy all day. He hardly slept at all. That didn't leave me any time to—how was my husband killed?" she asked, suddenly realizing that she couldn't remember if the detective had told her that or not. If he had, she'd blocked it out. But now she wanted to know.

Had Peter been shot, stabbed, strangled or mowed down by some vehicle? The very thought of each method made her want to shiver.

"You really don't want to know," Nick told her quietly.

"Yes, I do," she said emphatically. In a strange way, she felt she owed it to Peter to know all the details regarding his death. She could at least do that much for him.

"All right—just remember, you asked to hear this. Your husband was strangled," Nick told her crisply. "The medical examiner will give the official verdict, but from the looks of it, I'd say someone put a plastic bag over the sheriff's head and held it tight against his face until he suffocated."

Now she did shiver, visualizing the scenario in her mind. Peter might not have been the husband she'd always dreamed of, but he didn't deserve to die like that.

He didn't deserve to die at all, but to live a long life, being there for his son even if they weren't going to be there for each other much longer. She hoped he hadn't suffered.

"How do you know it was a plastic bag?" she asked. "Maybe someone just strangled him with their bare hands—or hung him." Each method she suggested just made it that much worse for her. But now that the detective was talking about it, she wanted all the details—and then she'd lock this subject away forever. She never wanted to revisit it for *any* reason.

"Well, for one thing, there were no dark ligature marks around his neck. If he was hung or manually strangled, there would have been telltale marks left around his neck."

Nick paused a moment, thinking of the card that had been found on the sheriff's person. Specifically, in his pocket. Similar cards, with something different written on each, were found on the other two men who had been dug up.

He considered withholding this from her, then

decided that it might be better out in the open. You never knew where something might lead.

"He had a card on him."

"A card?" she repeated, puzzled. "You mean like a playing card or a business card?"

"More like the kind that's used to print business cards, except that there was nothing printed on it except for just one word, and that was handwritten."

She didn't know why she instinctively braced herself, but she did. "What was the word?"

"Liar."

Suzy blinked and stared at him. Had he just accused her of lying? About what? "Excuse me?" she cried.

"That was the word written on the card—*liar*," he explained. "Would you know anyone who would accuse your husband of being a liar?"

She shook her head, painfully aware that she was no help in finding Peter's killer. The detective was probably tired of hearing her negative answers. But she couldn't exactly tell him what she didn't know.

"Can't think of a single person. As far as I know, Peter was regarded as a pillar of the community, a real good guy. I don't know of anyone who would accuse him of being a liar. Unless it was one of the women he was seeing," she amended. Now that she said it out loud, his "good guy" status was on shaky ground.

Suzy shrugged her shoulders again in a hapless gesture. "And, like I already told you, I don't even have any proof that he *was* seeing other women. It wasn't as if I'd found any love notes in his pockets, or any lipstick smeared on his collar. It was just a feeling I had," she admitted, "because things were so strained between us lately."

"Maybe that wasn't your fault," Nick suggested. When she glanced in his direction, confusion written on her features, he added, "Maybe the sheriff was acting that way because of whatever got him killed."

She supposed it was possible. But then, why hadn't Peter said something? Why had he shouldered this burden on his own?

A ragged sigh broke free as she finished changing the baby.

She looked at the detective, her eyes meeting his. Hers were guilt ridden. "He should have talked to me, told me what was going on."

"Maybe he just didn't want to burden you—or get you involved," Nick told her.

But she was already involved. She was his wife and this was where the words *for better or for worse* came into play.

Had she failed Peter?

She couldn't think about that now. If she let herself get mired in guilt, she wouldn't be of any use to Andy and right now, he was her top priority.

Replaying the detective's words in her head, Suzy suddenly realized something. With a now fresher-smelling Andy in her arms, she turned to look at the man who'd forced her into all this introspection.

"I take it that by saying that, you no longer find me to be a—how do they put it?" she asked, searching for the right terms. "A person of interest?" she recalled.

He wouldn't exactly say that, Nick thought. Not by a long shot. But since he didn't mean the phrase the same way she meant it, he refrained from making a direct comment on her question.

Even if he *did* find her person to be of interest.

Chapter 4

After a beat, Nick realized that the sheriff's widow was still waiting for an answer. "For now," he told her, "we're moving on."

"For now," she repeated.

Did that mean that he really *did* suspect her? The idea was utterly insane to her, but obviously not to him. The last thing she needed or wanted was to have that hanging over her head like some sword of Damocles. If nothing else, she wanted this absurd notion to be cleared up and gotten out of the way.

Now.

"Does that mean you're planning on revisiting your assumption that I had something to do with my husband's—" She couldn't even bring herself to say the word *murder,* much less contemplate the horrid act. How in heaven's name could this solemn detective possibly think she caused Peter's death? "Just for the record, Detective Jeffries, I draw the line at killing anything larger than a swarm of ants."

"Ants," he echoed, nodding. The barest hint of a smile threatened to curve his lips. "Can't stand them myself," he told her by way of agreement.

For a moment Nick watched her as she stood holding her baby, swaying to and fro ever so slightly to soothe him and keep him quiet. Unless he missed his guess, those were tears causing her eyes to glisten like that. He had a gut feeling that they were genuine, which in turn made him feel guilty for his questioning.

"Do you have anyone you'd like me to call?" Nick asked, his voice a great deal less stern than it had just been.

Her mind in turmoil, Suzy tried to make sense of the question. "You mean so you could question them about my marriage?"

Maybe he *had* been a bit too harsh on her. But

damn it, it was his job. He had to eliminate potential suspects, take in motives, opportunity and all the rest of it. Spouses killed their other halves more often than not.

Even so, he could feel guilt weighing heavily on him. And that was new. Cases—and the people involved in them—didn't, as a rule, get to him.

This woman was different. He'd sensed that even before he'd carried her into her house.

"No," he explained. "As in getting someone to come and stay here with you, maybe help you out with the baby while you try to pull yourself together."

She tossed her head, her long blond hair flying over the shoulder that wasn't currently occupied by her son. "Newsflash, Detective Jeffries, I *am* together."

Detective Jeffries sounded so formal, and although he usually liked maintaining that wall between a potential suspect and himself, he didn't this time.

"Call me Nick," he told her.

"Doesn't matter what I call you, 'Nick,' my answer's still going to be the same," she informed him.

He knew he should just back off. That any more

interaction with this woman would get him in deeper. He didn't want that. But somehow, he just couldn't make himself walk away yet, not when she looked as if the whole world had just exploded in on her—and he'd been the cause of her pain.

"Look, I meant no disrespect, but you are dealing with an emotional situation and taking care of a newborn isn't exactly a walk in the park, especially not when it's your first baby and you find yourself questioning every move you make, every thought you have." At this point, there was nothing but sympathetic understanding in Nick's voice. "I just asked if there is a friend or a relative I could call for you. Somebody for you to lean on if you needed to."

And this way, he thought, *I won't have to volunteer for the position.*

Suzy flushed. The man was trying to be nice to her, and she had all but bitten his head off. Maybe she really *was* going to pieces over this and didn't even realize it.

"Yes, there's someone," she admitted quietly. "My sister, Lori."

He waited a moment, thinking she would give him her sister's phone number. When she didn't, Nick prodded, "Can I have her number?"

"That's okay, I can call her," Suzy told him.

Maybe that wasn't such a bad idea, getting Lori to come, she thought. She could always count on Lori, just as Lori could always count on her. They were each other's support system. They always had been, going all the way back to the days when they had thought that all children had parents who fell asleep, fully clothed, on any flat surface that was handy, clutching a bottle of whiskey.

A little more than a year apart in age—with her being the older one—she and Lori were in tune to each other's feelings. It was Lori who had first sensed that she wasn't as happy in her marriage as she'd hoped to be. And it was Lori who'd made her promise that she would come to her if there was ever a problem.

This certainly qualified as a problem.

Since the woman wasn't making an attempt to walk over to the phone and pick it up, Nick made another offer. "I can hold the baby for you while you make your call."

She hadn't made a move yet because she was trying to find the right words to apologize to him. She supposed that saying "I'm sorry" was a one-size-fits-all catchall. It felt insufficient, but she used it anyway.

"I'm sorry." When she saw him raise a quizzical eyebrow, she added, "I know you were just trying to be nice and I just about bit your head off. I really didn't mean to—"

He smiled at her for the first time since she'd opened the door to him and his partner. Really smiled. Suzy caught herself thinking that he had a nice smile, one of those terrific boyish ones that utterly captivated the beholder and transformed his face.

Rather than an austere representative of the law, Nick Jeffries suddenly became human, someone she could relate to and even talk to.

"Don't worry about it," he told her. "My skin's a lot tougher than you think, Mrs. Burris."

"Suzy," she corrected. "Call me Suzy. Being called Mrs. Burris makes me feel like a gray-haired grandmother in sensible shoes."

He glanced down at her feet, noticing for the first time that she wasn't barefoot, the way his own wife used to be the minute she walked in through the front door. And rather than wearing something like comfortable slippers, Suzy had on high heels. Three-and-a-half or four-inch heels if he didn't miss his guess. She moved around so effortlessly in them, he'd just naturally *assumed* that the woman was barefoot.

But now that he'd looked—and, he had to admit, admired—he could see how very wrong he'd been. The shoes made her legs look sexy.

"Nothing sensible about *those* shoes," Nick commented with an appreciative grin. "Don't they bother your feet?" he asked.

She shook her head. "I don't even know I have them on."

The shoes had been one of her ways of coping with her situation. She gravitated toward pretty things, toward things that *made* her feel pretty and took her attention away—for however short a time—from whatever was bothering her.

When she'd been a teenager, she sought distractions to make her forget about her abusive parents, now she'd looked for distractions to make her momentarily forget about the husband who was pulling away from her. The husband who had never really made the "magic" happen for her, even in the beginning.

"They're my guilty pleasure," she explained.

"If you say so." Nick looked at the baby in her arms who was growing more and more vocal about his mounting unhappiness. "My offer still stands.

I can hold him for you while you call your sister. You might find it a little hard to talk with him crying like that."

The detective had a point, she thought. Pressing her lips together, she glanced from her son to Nick—and hesitated.

Nick could almost read her thoughts. "I do know how to hold a newborn."

There was no missing the confidence in his voice. "You have children, Detective—Nick?" she corrected herself at the last moment.

He thought of his ex-wife and the baby she'd chosen to erase from their lives without giving him the opportunity to voice his opinion, or even say a word in its defense. Just like that. It was gone before he even knew of its existence.

He'd found out quite by accident—looking for their bankbook, he'd come across the notification from a test that her gynecologist had run that Julie was pregnant. That was the afternoon he'd gone through a huge potpourri of emotions, all jumbled up and overlapping one another. But ultimately, the biggest emotion he experienced, was pure joy.

Elated at the news, he'd stopped off at his local bookstore during his lunch break and loaded up on every parenting book he could find, as well as a huge book singularly devoted to the selection of a name for the baby.

His head crammed full of plans for the baby-to-be, he came home only to discover that there was no need for plans at all. Julie had "gotten rid of the problem," to use her phraseology when he'd started talking about needing to move to a larger home in a better school district. Without a word to him, she'd swept away their unborn child as if it was some annoying, trivial inconvenience.

The discovery of what she'd done—leaving him out the way she had—left him reeling and destroyed the last drop of love that still existed. In effect it sounded the death knell of a marriage that was already staggering on its last legs.

"No," he answered Suzy quietly, "I don't have any children." Then, in case she had any further questions about his lack of family, he added, "I'm not married. But that doesn't mean I don't know how to hold a baby."

Then, as if to make his point, he gently took her son from her arms.

Nervous about surrendering Andy to this man, she was about to warn Nick not to let the baby's head drop back—or forward, But before she could get the words out, she saw that she had no need to coach him. The detective was holding her son far better and more comfortably than Peter had the handful of times that he'd made an attempt to act like a parent.

Suzy looked on in admiration and gave the detective his due. "You're a natural."

Nick blocked the bittersweet feeling unexpectedly filtering through him as he held this tiny miracle in his arms. Even so, he couldn't help wondering what it would have been like had he learned about his baby in time to talk his ex into having it. Who knew the kind of turn his life might have taken?

He glanced away from the baby for an instant. "You sound surprised."

Andy had settled down. The infant seemed to be fascinated by this new person holding him. "I don't really think of police detectives as having nurturing instincts," Suzy confessed.

Nick smiled down at the infant who was staring at him and seemed to be all eyes at the moment. "Maybe you should think about changing your opinion about members of the police force," he suggested.

She thought he was serious until she saw the amused glint in his eyes.

"Maybe," she agreed. Rousing herself—his eyes had a definite hypnotic effect—she said, "I won't be long," and walked out of the living room.

There was a phone in the kitchen and she made her way toward it. There was another extension in the living room, where she had just been with Andy and Nick, but she wanted a little privacy. It wasn't that she had anything secretive to share with Lori. She just wanted to be able to break down if it came to that.

Lori would understand.

This detective would just think of her as being weak, and she didn't feel like being judged right now. Her last shred of bravado and defensiveness had been used up. She had nothing to shield herself with, no weapons close at hand to help her deflect any unwanted criticism—or pity for that matter.

She might not have been in love with Peter, but his totally unexpected, sudden death, had left her shaken and confused about the immediate future.

She didn't like feeling this way, didn't like the vulnerability, and until she could get herself under control—until she could feel that she was *back* in control of her life—she wanted to be able to talk to her sister without anyone overhearing her.

Because they were so in tune to one another

due to the bond they'd shared growing up in their less-than-idyllic nurturing household, Lori knew something was wrong the instant she heard Suzy utter her name.

It was the *way* she said it. "Lori?"

"Suzy? What's wrong? Why are you calling?" Lori asked. The next second she'd jumped to her own conclusion. "Is it the baby, Suzy? Is there something wrong with Andy?"

It was hard to keep her voice from shaking. Somehow, she managed, although she wouldn't have been able to say just how. "No, it's not Andy."

"You? Do you need to go back to the hospital? I told you that you checked yourself out too soon. Another day or two with nurses close by to help wouldn't have killed you," her sister protested.

It took a couple of seconds before Suzy could get a word in edgewise. "I'm fine, Lori." But that wasn't strictly true, she upbraided herself silently. "That is, there's nothing wrong with me. At least, nothing physical." God, this was coming out all wrong, she thought in despair.

Her words led her sister to the only remaining option. "Is it Peter?"

Suzy closed her eyes. She could feel an emptiness forming within her. But, if she were being honest with herself, that emptiness had been there before Peter's death. She'd just worked hard at ignoring it.

But that wasn't possible anymore.

"Yes," she answered, the word all but sticking in her throat.

Suzy heard her sister sigh on the other end of the line. Lori, as loyal as the day was long, reacted to Peter according to the information she gleaned from her, and at present, because she *had* shared her feelings that Peter had been growing more and more distant with her, Lori was not too keen on her brother-in-law.

"All right, Suzy, out with it. What's the almighty sheriff of the county done now?" Lori asked.

She felt disloyal to Peter because of the image Lori had of him, thanks to her, and hypocritical at the same time because she just couldn't pretend that she actually loved the man. That had ended way *before* the baby had been born.

"He died," she told Lori, her voice flat and devoid of any emotion.

There was a pause on the other end. Finally, her sister said, "Suzy, I think there's something wrong with the connection we have. I thought I just heard you say that Peter—"

"He died," Suzy repeated in the same flat, dis-embodied voice. The words sounded so strange, so stilted, to her ear. Swallowing, she forced more words out of her mouth. "Peter's dead, Lori."

"How? When?" Lori cried in utter disbelief.

"The police detectives who came to the house said that someone suffocated Peter yesterday." Guilt shot through her with sharp, fresh arrows, piercing her conscience if not her heart. "Oh, Lori, I was waiting up all night for him—"

"Because you were worried," her sister ended her sentence for her. They'd always been able to do that with each other, second-guess what the other was going to say. Except for this time.

"No, Lori. Because I was going to ask him for a divorce. That's what makes this so much worse. Peter might have been fighting for his life at the very moment that I was sitting here, trying to fig-ure out just how to finally tell him that I was leav-ing him, that I wanted a divorce."

Lori heard the pain, the heavy sting of guilt in her sister's voice and she ached for Suzy.

"It's not your fault, you know, Suz," she told her. "Not your fault he's dead."

Suzy blew out an unsteady breath. "I know. But I still feel guilty."

"Don't," her sister ordered, then added, "I'll be there as soon as I can. Hang in there, Suzy. Everything's going to be all right," Lori promised just before she hung up.

Suzy stared at the phone receiver in her hand. "Everything wasn't all right before this happened," Suzy said quietly, more to herself than to the sister who was no longer there.

She didn't remember hanging up the phone. It was in her hand one minute, then back in the cradle the next. She stared at it in surprise.

Get a grip! she ordered herself.

Taking a deep breath, Suzy squared her shoulders, turned around and walked back into the living room, placing one foot in front of the other numbly. It was all that she could do.

She was just in time to see Andy spit up on the detective's jacket.

Rushing over, she scooped up the baby, taking Andy from him with one arm while offering Nick a cloth wipe that she had left draped on the arm of the sofa.

"I'm so sorry," she apologized with feeling. "If you take that off, I can clean it for you so that the stain doesn't set."

Though being christened with recycled milk

didn't particularly upset him—he'd had worse things hurled at his clothing—Nick regarded her offer to clean his jacket rather dubiously.

"You have a dry cleaner out back?" he quipped.

She placed Andy into the playpen she had set up in the living room. The infant fussed for a moment, then began playing with his feet, which were still a source of utter fascination for him.

"No," she replied to Nick as she held her hand out for his jacket, "but I got pretty good at getting all sorts of stubborn stains out of clothes when I was growing up."

Nick came to the only logical conclusion he could with the information he'd been given. "You were a tomboy?" he asked. He shrugged out of the jacket and folded it so that the stain was on top before he handed it over to Suzy.

"No, I had parents who made falling down in a drunken stupor wherever they might happen to be into pretty much of a way of life."

She said it so matter-of-factly, he thought she was just being flippant. But one look into her eyes told him she was serious.

The woman had led one hell of a life in her relatively short time on earth.

For the second time within an hour, he felt the

very definite, strong stirrings of protectiveness rising to the surface.

He did what he could to block them.

Chapter 5

"There you go," Suzy said, emerging from the laundry room roughly fifteen minutes later. She presented Nick with his jacket. "I did manage to get the stain out, and once that section dries—" she pointed it out to him "—there shouldn't be any telltale evidence that my son decided to use your jacket as his napkin. If you still want to take it to the cleaners anyway, I'll be more than happy to pay the bill."

Nick looked the jacket over carefully, clearly impressed. He couldn't detect even a trace of the milky substance that had decorated his shoulder a short while ago.

At this point, all that remained was just the faintest hint of a damp spot, and that looked as if it was disappearing, as well.

"How did you do that?" he marveled. He had a razor-sharp mind when it came to solving crimes. Common everyday things, though, like cooking or doing laundry, turned out to be far more of a challenge for him than he was happy about.

Suzy looked at him with an utterly serious expression. "I don't usually give away my secrets."

Maybe the woman was trying to get a patent on the process. It certainly had performed a minor miracle on his jacket. "Oh, well then—"

The serious expression was instantly gone, replaced by a suppressed laugh. Suzy put her hand on his arm to keep him from withdrawing. She'd always been a toucher when she spoke to people. It was one of the things that had attracted Peter to her in the first place—and one of the first things he'd objected to once they were married. He didn't like her touching other people. And by "other people" he'd meant men.

"I was just kidding," she said quickly. "The secret is just getting to the stain fast, before it sets, and then soaking the area with lemon juice."

He had to have heard her wrong. Was she talking about cleaning something or cooking it? "Lemon juice?"

She nodded. "Lemon juice. You'd be surprised at how good it is at getting out all sorts of stains—including blood."

"Blood," he repeated, wondering just how she'd found that out. "I'll have to remember that the next time someone shoots me," he said drolly.

Nick slipped on his jacket again. As he did so, he glanced down at his watch. He'd been here far longer than he'd intended for an initial interview, but even so, he was rather reluctant to leave the woman alone like this. And then he suddenly remembered that he had to call the precinct to have a car sent for him since Juarez took off in the one they normally shared.

"Excuse me a minute," he said to Suzy as he took his cellphone out of his pocket and turned away from her to make the call.

The moment he pressed the last number, someone immediately came on, needlessly identifying themselves as "Dispatch."

"Dispatch, this is Detective Jeffries. I need a

car sent to Sheriff Burris's house." Pausing to listen to the question being asked of him, he replied, "Because Juarez's wife went into early labor, and I let him have the car so he could get to the hospital, that's why. Now I need to requisition another car so that I can get back to the station house and start digging through some paperwork."

The detective, Suzy thought, didn't sound very happy about having to explain himself. He struck her as someone who was accustomed to following his own rules, going his own way, without being subjected to questions.

"How long?" she heard him ask sharply. From the impatient noise he made, she took it to mean that "how long?" had suddenly translated into "too long."

Suzy thought for a moment, made up her mind quickly and then planted herself directly in front of the detective to get his attention. He looked at her quizzically.

"I can drive you there," she mouthed to him, not wanting her voice to interfere with the voice that he was listening to on his cellphone.

"Hold on a minute, Gus," Nick told dispatch. Covering the lower portion of his phone, he addressed his question to Suzy. "What?"

Because her throat suddenly felt hoarse out of the blue, she cleared it before she spoke up. "I can take you to the station."

He'd just told the woman her husband was murdered, and then all but accused her of being behind the crime before he'd decided that she could be ruled out. That was more than enough for anyone to handle in one day. He had no intention of imposing on Suzy Burris any further—at least not unless he had absolutely no other choice.

Nick waved away her offer. "That's all right, I can have—"

"No, really, I insist," she said a little more forcefully, although she made sure that she maintained a friendly expression on her face. "The fresh air might do me some good. I've been in the house for going on two days straight and I'm coming down with cabin fever."

Nick looked over toward the playpen where Andy was still finding his extremities to be utterly fascinating entities. "What about your son?"

"He's too young for cabin fever," she told him matter-of-factly.

Nick completely missed the humor in her eyes. "No, I mean what are you going to do with him while you're driving me?"

"Andy has a car seat," she assured Nick. "And I've already taken him on road trips, so yours won't be the first. He's very accommodating." Thank God she had Andy, she thought. He made everything worthwhile, even if he had wreaked havoc on her hormones. "Of course," she speculated, looking over toward her son, "he doesn't talk yet, so that might change once he thinks he has a say in matters."

Her banter didn't distract him from his concerns. "Are you sure you're up to it?"

"Up to it?" she echoed with a small laugh that wasn't altogether laced with humor. "I'd say I pretty much *need* it." She paused for a moment, taking a breath before continuing to try to convince the detective. "A little fresh air might help me clear my head. And this way, I'll have a direction instead of driving around aimlessly, so you'll actually be doing me a favor."

He watched Suzy for a long moment, debating whether or not to believe her. Finally, he inclined his head. "If you put it that way, I guess I can't turn the offer down." Removing his hand from his cellphone's mouthpiece, he changed his instructions to dispatch. "Cancel the car, Gus. I've just managed to hitch a ride." Terminating the call, he closed his phone, looked at her and smiled. "Whenever you're ready," he told her, letting his voice trail off.

She nodded. "Just let me get a coat and an extra blanket for Andy." For the beginning of February, it was unseasonably warm, but this was still winter and she wasn't about to take any chances on her son catching a chill if the temperature suddenly dropped.

She'd crossed to the stairs to get the items when the doorbell chimed and stopped her in her tracks. Backtracking, she went to the front door. But as she was about to open it, she heard Nick shout out a warning, "Suzy, don't!" then suddenly found herself being physically blocked from the door because Nick had put himself in between her and it.

"Have you lost your mind?" she demanded. She nearly stumbled and fell backward because of the body block, and most likely would have, had Nick not grabbed her arm to steady her. "What the hell was that all about?" she cried, utterly stunned.

Was he trying to keep her sister out, after telling her to call Lori over?

Nick realized that it was a woman standing on the doorstep, a petite blonde who resembled the sheriff's widow.

This had to be the sister, he thought, feeling

somewhat relieved. Lowering his guard, he allowed himself to relax a little.

"You have to be more careful about answering the door," he told her.

"Any particular reason why?" Suzy asked, a hint of sarcasm in her voice.

He didn't want to frighten her or add to her burden, but it was better for her to be cautious than sorry.

"Your husband wasn't the only one killed yesterday. He was one of three. Now if his death was a random killing, or one that was carefully planned with the other two murders thrown in to throw people off the trail, I don't know. But until we sort it all out, I'd say it was better to ask the person to identify themselves before opening your door."

Oh, Peter, what have you done? "Then you think that my son and I might be in danger?" she asked before Lori could ask the same question.

"There's a possibility," he allowed. "Until I start getting some straight answers, I really can't tell you what it is you might be up against."

Worried about what she had inadvertently dragged her sister into, Suzy told her, "Then maybe you shouldn't stay here with me."

Lori was cut out of the same fabric as she was.

"My place is here with you and my nephew. Just *try* to get me to stay away," Lori dared her. Turning, she gave the man her sister had been talking to a thorough once-over. "Hi, I'm Lori, Suzy's sister."

Nick took the hand she offered, closing his over it. The women more than just looked alike. They obviously had the same temperament.

"I kind of figured that out," he told her warmly. He looked back at Suzy. "Forget about driving me," he said. "Stay here with your sister, try to get a decent night's sleep if you can. I'll be back tomorrow—or the day after," he qualified. He had no idea how the rest of the investigations were going and always wanted to leave space for adjustment in case the feds had other leads that were more pressing. When he saw the confused expression in Suzy's eyes, he explained, "I have more questions I need to ask you."

Although Peter's death was still very much of a shock to her, she was beginning to regain control over herself, beginning to find her way back to even ground. But the last thing she needed right now was to be left wondering what else would be unearthed about her husband. If the detective had more questions, she wanted to hear them now, not spend the next twelve or so hours anticipating them.

"I doubt if I'm going to be able to fall asleep at all tonight, much less get a decent night's sleep, so unless you have to be somewhere else right now, you might as well get started asking those other questions, Detective. Although," she reminded him, "I'm really not sure how much of a help I'm going to be. Like I said earlier, Peter didn't exactly bring his work home with him."

"Literally?" he asked.

She had no idea what Nick actually meant by that. "Excuse me?"

"Literally," he repeated. Seeing that she was still puzzled, he elaborated on the question. "Did the sheriff bring home any files, a briefcase he might have carried back and forth with him. A laptop computer he kept locked up somewhere?"

The answer to all but the last question was yes. "Peter turned the guest bedroom into his office," she volunteered. "Anything he brought home I guess would be there. He never left any of that anywhere else in the house."

A home office. Maybe now they were finally getting somewhere. "Do I have your permission to go through it?" Nick asked.

Peter was gone, there was no longer a need to protect his things, she thought.

"Sure, if it'll help you find out who killed Peter. But first," she cautioned, "you're going to have to get into it."

It was Nick's turn to be confused and say, "Excuse me?"

Before she could explain, the baby began fussing again. Suzy looked toward the playpen, torn.

"Go, I've got this," Lori told her, waving her sister off as she went to get her nephew out of the playpen.

"Thanks," Suzy said to her sister, then beckoned for the detective to come with her. "It's this way," she told him, leading the way to the room in question. "Peter keeps—kept—" she corrected herself "—his office locked up. When I asked him about it once, he said that it was to make sure that if anyone ever broke into the house, they wouldn't be able to get into what he called 'sensitive' material."

Nick wondered if that was just a term the sheriff had bandied about to make himself seem important, or if it actually stood for something.

"Any idea what that was?" he asked her.

Suzy stopped before the closed door and shook her head. "Not a clue."

Nick regarded the door for a long moment. It didn't look particularly reinforced. Why the drama?

"You realize that anyone who could break into the house could easily break into this room, as well," he pointed out.

The weary smile that curved the corners of her mouth told Nick that the sheriff's widow was well aware of that.

"The way I saw it," she told Nick, "whatever Peter had in there was something he didn't want me to see. Can't say I wasn't curious," she admitted, then shrugged indifferently, "but then I thought that maybe it was like Pandora's box— once it was opened, the things that I'd find there could never be put back and life might never be the same again. I decided not to risk it.

"But I can't say I liked him having secrets like that. It really bothered me. A lot." She looked at Nick. "It's one of the reasons I decided to divorce him," she confessed with a sigh. "There were just too many secrets."

Whatever she could tell him might just make his job that much easier. "What were some of the others?"

"The usual things." When he looked at her,

waiting, she elaborated. "Hang-ups when I would answer the phone. More and more late nights out. Inconsistencies in the things he told me."

"Such as?" he prodded.

"Such as why he left the Dallas police force." That was the biggest inconsistency—she didn't want to call it a lie, but in her heart, she knew it had to be. Or at least, that one of the reasons—if not more—that he'd given her was a lie. "When he first told me about it, Peter just shrugged it off, said he felt it was just time for him to make a move, to try something different.

"Another time he said that he left because he felt there were just too many corrupt cops on the force and rather than turn on them—and risk getting killed himself—he just resigned.

"And then there was the time he ran into someone he knew from Dallas," she continued. She wasn't aware that her expression hardened somewhat—but Nick was. "I overheard the other man saying something about Peter having to disappear quickly because of some kind of scandal he was involved in."

Nick made a note to look up the sheriff's record with the Dallas Police Department. "Do you know who the other man was?"

She shook her head. "Never saw him before—or after. When I asked Peter if his friend was coming back, he cut me off by saying the man wasn't a friend, he was just an acquaintance from the department. He seemed pretty upset, so I didn't press the matter." Suzy shook her head. She couldn't help wondering if any of this was her fault. If she could have done something differently to keep Peter from getting killed. "Maybe I should have."

"You wouldn't have known if he was telling you the truth or not, anyway," Nick pointed out. "That's the trouble with someone who keeps changing his story."

Suzy nodded sadly. "I know." She indicated the locked door that was keeping them from looking through Peter's things. "Do you want me to call a handyman to take that off its hinges?"

He didn't view the locked door as an obstacle. "No need," he told her. "I'm kind of handy myself." But rather than taking the hinges off, Nick merely took out his wallet and extracted two very thin looking metal tools. Using both, he inserted them into door's keyhole and swiftly began working the lock.

Glancing at Suzy over his shoulder, he asked,

"I've got your permission to unlock the door, right?"

The gesture she used told him to have at it. "Be my guest."

Before she'd uttered the last word, Nick already had the door unlocked and was turning the doorknob to enter the room.

Suzy was suitably impressed at how effortlessly the detective had managed that. "They teach cat burglary at the police academy?" she asked, amused.

"No, they don't. That particular skill comes under the heading of extracurricular activity," he answered with as straight a face as he could manage. "It's something—if you're lucky—that you pick up along the way from the criminals you wind up arresting."

Once in the room, Nick looked around slowly. His first impression was that there was nothing outstanding about the room, nothing to set it apart or make it appear special. It was just another bedroom converted into a home office.

The man did have a very large desk. Was that to convey his importance, or did he just favor large writing areas? It definitely dominated the room, but the surface of the alder wood desk was completely devoid of any papers despite the fact that there was a laser printer set up right next to a computer tower. Both were turned off.

On the far side of the desk, standing next to it, was a professional-looking shredding machine. Its container, Nick noticed, was partially filled. He crossed to that first.

Removing the much heavier top portion, he found that the paper inside the container was shredded to the point that it would take a team of dedicated experts, working nonstop for several days, before they could even hope to begin to attempt to re-create the pages that had been fed through the machine's sharp teeth. And even after that, it wasn't a foregone conclusion that there could be anything gleaned from that effort.

Why would a sheriff of a county need that kind of a shredder? Just what was the man shredding and why?

Leaving that puzzle for later, Nick turned to the computer next. He hit the power button and waited for the tower to reboot. When it finished going through its paces, a picture came together on the screen.

"Interesting screen saver," Nick commented as he studied it.

Peter had never had the computer on around her. Curious, she took a look and saw that the screen saver was comprised of an army of dollar signs marching off into infinity.

She wasn't surprised. "Peter always had a weakness for money," she told the detective. "He complained more than once that he didn't feel he was getting paid what he deserved." Already the marching dollar signs were getting on her nerves. "Can you get into it?"

The computer was, as he expected, password protected. "This is a little trickier than unlocking a door," he told her. "But then again, a lot of people elect to go with things they can easily remember. What's the date that you got married?" he asked.

She sincerely doubted that Peter would use that. That would indicate that he was sentimental about the date and she knew that he wasn't.

But she gave the date to Nick anyway and he typed it in.

The second he hit Enter the words *Wiping out hard drive* appeared. Below it was a sixty second countdown.

And they already had just forty-five seconds left.

And then they had forty-four.

Chapter 6

"I can't stop it." Nick was acutely aware that the seconds were ticking away.

His fingers flew across the keyboard and he was using every trick he could think of, but nothing was working.

The countdown continued. The seconds were slipping away.

"Damn it," he muttered in frustration.

And then, with three seconds left to go, the screen suddenly went blank. There was no telltale sound, no indication that anything was being destroyed. He had no idea what had happened but it appeared that the crisis had been averted.

How?

Had this countdown been some kind of elaborate hoax? Nick knew that, with all his desperate typing, he still hadn't come up with the right combination of keys needed to save the information.

So why had the screen gone blank?

"I did it?" It was more of a question than a triumphant boast, directed at the universe in general.

As he turned toward the sheriff's widow to vocalize his confusion, it suddenly became clear.

"You did it," Nick amended, almost amused at how simple the solution had been.

Suzy stood there with a smile on her face—and the computer power plug in her hand. She had pulled it out of the wall socket, causing the computer to stop its destructive activity and just shut off.

Why hadn't he thought of that?

"Quick thinking," he complimented her.

"Basic thinking," she corrected. She looked at the plug before placing it on the table beside the tower. "Actually, it's the only kind of thinking I'm capable of—I don't know that much about computers, I just know that the ones that aren't the portable kind that run on batteries need a power source. I got caught in a blackout once and the term paper I was working on disappeared because the computer shut down the moment the power stopped flowing through it." A slight smile curved her lips. "Knew that hard-learned lesson would come in handy someday."

Had she shut off the computer's power source fast enough? Nick wondered as he regarded the dark computer screen.

"I certainly hope so," he muttered out loud.

"So now what?" she asked, nodding at the tower. "Are you going to bring it to some tech expert in the police department?"

"We don't have one of those in Vengeance." At least, none that he was aware of. "But the FBI does." The FBI had everything available to them. It was a matter of knowing who to ask. He'd never been very good at taking hat in hand and pleading his case, though.

"The FBI?" she asked incredulously. Did they even have a satellite office out here? "You can do that? Just walk in and bring a computer to them?"

"Probably not under normal circumstances," he conceded, but God knew this case didn't fit under that heading. "But right now, there's a local police/FBI joint task force working on the murders."

"Murders," she echoed. For a moment, she'd forgotten that Peter's death was not an isolated incident. She really didn't know if that made it better or worse. "If other people were killed, maybe Peter's death was just collateral damage. You know, wrong place, wrong time, that sort of thing. Maybe the killer didn't want to leave a witness behind."

"You're forgetting about the card that was found in your husband's pocket." He looked at her, wishing that for her sake, he could say that her theory was right. But it wasn't. Burris had been singled out, just the way the other two men had been. "This was personal."

A thought occurred to her. A horrible, crushing thought. "Could Peter have gotten the other two people killed?" she asked. "Could they have been unwilling witnesses to *his* death, and then the killer eliminated them, too, to keep them from talking?"

There was only one thing wrong with her theory. "The other men had cards on them, too."

Suzy steepled her hands before her lips, covering them, holding back the sound of anguished distress that had risen to them and was still hovering there.

"Then it *is* a serial killer," she cried. How many more people were going to have to die before this monster was caught?

"We're not ready to say that yet," Nick cautioned, fervently hoping that wasn't the case. "The last thing we need is having the public panic on us. We want to keep them in the dark as long as possible—in case we're wrong and this is just part of some elaborate vendetta."

She ran her hands up and down her arms, feeling a definite chill though the temperature inside the house hadn't changed. She could feel her nerves go on high alert.

"Are my son and I in any danger?" she asked.

Nick gave it to her straight and was as honest with her as he could. "I don't think so. The killer seemed exclusively focused on the three people he killed."

But maybe the killing would be extended to the victims' families.

Get a grip, Suzy. You can't let yourself think that way.

She was struck by something Nick had just said.

"Then you know it was a man who killed Peter and the others?"

"Actually, no, I don't," he admitted. "It's just an assumption. Most multiple killers tend to be men," he told her. "And given the people who were murdered, it would have had to have been a fairly strong woman to get them all out there and bury them. Process of elimination says it's most likely a man," he concluded.

Suzy kept going back to the other two men in her mind. She needed answers. Were they friends of Peter's? People he dealt with?

"Can you tell me who else was killed, or are their identities something that's being kept from the public for the time being?" she asked.

"You'll know soon enough. We have to make sure all the families are contacted first." The FBI was handling that part of it, the part that involved handling the media and releasing information. The names were going to be released sooner than later, because of the media that had converged on Vengeance, thanks to the Grayson disappearance and probable kidnapping. The reporters were everywhere, digging into everything. Suzy was going to hear about the other two men soon enough, but he could talk to her later about the details.

"I understand, Detective."

"Did the sheriff ever talk about anyone in particular? Did he discuss his personal affairs with you?" Nick asked.

There was no humor in the small laugh that escaped her lips. "Peter actually talked less and less to me in the last six months or so. I think he'd started to have real regrets about talking me into getting pregnant and having a baby."

"If you don't mind my asking, why did you?" She didn't strike him as the type who would blindly do anything her husband asked her to—unless she wanted to. "Let him talk you into having a baby?" he explained when she seemed confused.

Her initial reaction had been to say no, but then she'd changed her mind.

"Because I felt I owed it to the marriage to give it another try," she told him honestly. "And I thought that maybe a baby would help us find that spark. The one I never seemed to have felt," she confessed, then pressed her lips together as her words replayed themselves in her head.

"I guess that's a little too much information." Suzy laughed ruefully, embarrassed over what she'd just admitted to a total stranger. He had a sympathetic look in his eyes, but she didn't want his sympathy. There was no reason to have allowed that slip out. It was much too personal. "That's certainly not going to help you solve the crime. Any of them," she tacked on.

"Technically, I'm only working your husband's murder," he told her. "We have the other two murders assigned to other people and we're sharing information—if there's any to share," he qualified. It was still early in the investigation and so far nothing was being shared. "Do you know if your husband kept any files or extraneous information around somewhere? You know, things that weren't on the computer, but he still didn't want anyone else to see?"

As he spoke, he started to conduct a search himself. He pulled at the middle drawer, only to find that it wouldn't budge. He looked down, his expression registering only mild surprise. "Did he always keep his desk locked?"

"I wouldn't know. Peter didn't want me in here." She knew how that had to sound, but she'd really had no interest in his work, other than it helped pay his share of the bills.

"How about when he was at work?" His guess was that most women would have taken the opportunity to poke around then. "Weren't you curious?" he prodded.

"Not really. Peter kept the office door locked. Besides, I was at work myself for most of that time." She paused a moment, then added, "I told myself that whatever he had in this room had to do with the job."

"And did you believe yourself?" Nick asked, watching her closely to get a handle on what she was really feeling.

She looked at him knowingly. "I'm not an idiot, Detective."

"No, ma'am," he agreed. "In my opinion, you're definitely not an idiot." He ended the sentence on a firm, upbeat note, waiting for her to follow it up with something, anything.

He didn't have long to wait.

"I felt that as long as I didn't ask questions and accuse him of cheating—as long as I supposedly didn't know what he was up to, we could make our way back from there, save the marriage. Maybe start over, for Andy's sake." But that hope had quickly died when Peter made himself even more scarce. He'd left her no choice but to ask for a divorce.

She blew out a long, heavy breath. "Now there's

no need to start over, at least, not with Peter." She looked up at the detective. "But I certainly will be starting over, won't I?"

He felt her discomfort. The woman had been through the wringer today. Nick made a quick decision. "I think I have enough here for now." He nodded at the computer tower. "I can come back tomorrow. And I am sorry for your loss, Mrs. Burris."

A bittersweet smile curved her mouth. "My loss, Detective, happened long before today—or yesterday." She watched as he took the various plugs and cables off, uncoupling the computer tower from the monitor and all the other peripheral bells and whistles that comprised its accessories. "You need any help with that?" she asked, indicating the tower.

He picked it up from the desk and tucked it under his arm. Nick couldn't help grinning at the offer. He was a good six feet tall with a solid athletic build while she was—what?—five-two, five-three and slight? The thought of her offering to help him carry *anything* amused him.

"Thanks," he told her, "but I think I can manage."

Of course he could, she thought wryly. "I'll walk you to the door."

He was about to say that he could find his own way out, then decided against it. Instead, he just nodded and said, "Thanks."

She was a nice woman, he thought. And, from what he was piecing together, she seemed *too* nice for the likes of the deceased sheriff.

Suzy stopped at the front door, opening it for him. "Do you have any idea when I can…pick up Peter's body?" That sounded so bizarre to her. Peter's body. A man like Peter should have had at least another forty years ahead of him, not cut down so soon. "For the funeral," she explained.

"The medical examiner has to complete his autopsy first." Because they had no medical examiner of their own, the department had requested one be brought in from Dallas. A J. D. Cameron arrived an hour ago, looking none too happy about being temporarily transplanted. "He probably won't be releasing any of the bodies for at least another day or so," he told her. "Best guess," he qualified, since he had no idea exactly how things worked in this formerly sleepy little town.

There'd never been a murder here before, at least not since it had been officially christened

"Vengeance" and incorporated. Legend had it, though, that the town's name came as a result of someone taking their revenge and killing a guilty party.

Suzy took the detective's qualification into account. She was about to say goodbye when he stopped and put the tower down on the front porch.

"Did you forget something, Detective?" she asked.

Nick dug into his pocket and took out one of the cards that he'd had made up for himself when he accepted this job—Vengeance, it turned out, didn't have "money to waste" on trivial things like business cards for its police detectives.

Maybe that should have warned him about the kind of place where he'd decided to settle down. But it had seemed like a good idea at the time. Besides, all things considered, he honestly didn't have a better place to be.

"I wanted to give you my card in case you happen to think of something before I come back tomorrow—or if you just want to talk—you can reach me at either one of these two numbers," he told her, pointing to the two phone numbers printed in the lower right-hand corner.

Accepting his card, Suzy looked at it as she nodded in response to what he had just said. "Thank you," she murmured.

Why did the sound of her voice, lowered like that, sound so incredibly sexy to him just now? Maybe, instead of jumping from one police force to another, he should have first gone on an extended vacation, somewhere peaceful where it would have been only him and several seashells?

"Yeah, well, I'll see you tomorrow," he mumbled. Turning on his heel, Nick made his way to the car one of his colleagues had dropped off for him. He noted absently that the vehicle was in desperate need of a wash.

He glanced up at the sky, wondering if it was going to rain. That would solve his problem and the countryside could certainly use a little rain these days. The land was rather parched. The summer had been a hot one and for the most part, there had been no relief except for an occasional anemic sprinkle.

He was doing it again, Nick suddenly realized as he popped the rear hood and put the computer tower inside the trunk. He was filling his mind—crowding it—with trivial information. It was a habit he'd developed years ago, a way to keep from thinking about what was *really* on his mind.

In this case, it should have been on details about the sheriff's murder. But it wasn't. Instead, his head was filled with extraneous details about the sheriff's widow. Those light blue eyes that had gotten to him.

He caught himself thinking that for a woman who'd given birth two months ago, she certainly had regained one hell of a figure. That in turn made him wonder what kind of a fool the sheriff must have been, to go tomcatting around when he had *that* waiting for him at home.

Some men didn't deserve the luck they had, he thought darkly.

He pulled himself up short. This was *not* where his head was supposed to be. What the hell was wrong with him, anyway? Nick silently demanded, upbraiding himself as he drove away from the house.

He had a murder to investigate and solve, a murder that could hold the key to the other two murders. And he certainly wasn't going to come to any definite conclusions thinking about that little blonde.

That way only led to trouble and he knew it.

"He seemed really nice," Lori said to her sister the second Suzy walked back into the living room.

"Are you going to call him?" she asked, indicating the card Suzy had in her hand.

Suzy let the card drop on the coffee table. "No. I don't have any more information to give him, other than what I already told him."

Lori sighed, shaking her head. "I wasn't thinking about you giving him *that* kind of information, Suzy," she said pointedly.

Stunned, Suzy could only stare at her sister. All right, so even if she wasn't in love with Peter, and hadn't been for a long time, there were still nice times to remember. "Lori, Peter's not even cold yet."

Lori rolled her eyes. "Honey, from what you told me, Peter's been cold for a real long time." She shrugged. "But you know me, I don't like to speak ill of the dead—"

"Then don't," Suzy said angrily.

Her tone fell on deaf ears. "—but Peter was never right for you."

Suzy didn't feel she was emotionally equipped to hear this right now. "Lori, I know you're just being loyal to me and all that, but trust me, honey, now just isn't the time for this."

Lori nibbled on her lower lip, looking very indecisive, as if she was debating with herself on whether or not to say something.

"I never told you this, Suzy, but Peter made a play for me about a month before you gave birth to the handsomest nephew in the world." Unable to continue with the topic, she'd opted for humor—except everyone wasn't laughing.

Suzy was speechless for a second. When she found her voice, it came out in a quiet whisper. "Why didn't you tell me?"

"Because I didn't want to hurt you, Suzy. Because I told him that because he was married to you and you were having his baby, I was going to pretend that he never made a move on me, but I warned him that if I ever heard that he was cheating on you, I was going to tell you that he propositioned me—and then I was going to vivisect him, cutting out one piece at a time."

"You threatened him? Oh, God," she cried, thinking of what the FBI could do with that. She knew that Lori was all talk, nothing more, but no one else did. "Lori, what were you *thinking?* He was the sheriff, for God's sake," she cried.

"Being sheriff certainly didn't make him perfect," Lori said sarcastically.

"No," Suzy agreed quietly, "it certainly didn't.

And for the record, Lori," she added in a more quiet tone, "I knew that Peter was cheating on me. I had no tangible proof," she admitted, "but I *knew*."

Chapter 7

It wasn't that Nick didn't trust the FBI, or that he'd once worked on the Dallas police force—because he hadn't.

The Houston Police Department had been the only one he'd served on before coming here, but Dallas was closer to Vengeance than Houston was—only forty miles away—and he liked being hands-on when it came to conducting an investigation. Had he had the option, he would have preferred working within his own department, but the Vengeance police department had some lamentable gaping holes when it came to being able to offer comprehensive services.

From what he'd observed recently, the officer who doubled as a tech advisor on the force knew about as much as he did about computers. Right now, Nick needed an expert. Preferably one he both knew and trusted.

And he knew and trusted someone in Dallas.

So, rather than heading back with the late sheriff's computer to the Vengeance precinct, Nick drove the extra forty miles and made his way into the crime investigation section within the Dallas police station.

He stopped long enough to sign in with the desk sergeant and requested "professional courtesy." After the stocky man had checked him out, Nick was escorted down into the bowels of the building in order to see Chester Bigelow, a tech expert he'd gotten to know when they had worked for the Houston police department at the same time that he was there.

Nick found the man in the break room, enjoying the last of what appeared to be a triple-decker Reuben sandwich, one of Bigelow's "guilty pleasures" as he liked to refer to it. Consumption of the latter was also one of the things that had earned Bigelow the nickname "Big." In appearance, he was anything but. Nick had often maintained that the man had a tapeworm. No matter what he ate, Bigelow remained as skinny as the proverbial rail.

Sensing another presence in the heretofore empty break room, the computer tech looked up from the article in the technical journal he'd been reading. A surprised smile replaced the neutral expression on his face when he recognized who was in the room with him.

"Look what the cat dragged in," Bigelow cried, grinning. "Nick Jeffries." And then his attention shifted to the computer tower that his old friend was cradling in his arms. "You know, they've got these newfangled things called laptops now. They're a hell of a lot easier to carry around. You might think about getting one."

Nick placed the tower down on the table in front of Bigelow. "I need your help, Big."

"That's what they all say," Bigelow responded with a laugh. "What's the matter, the lab tech in your department can't be browbeaten?"

Nick didn't waste any time with long explanations. "The lab tech in my department doesn't have as much computer savvy in his whole body as you do in your little finger."

Bigelow nodded, making no pretense at any false modesty. He knew he was good. Damn good. "Flattery. You must be desperate."

Nick saw no reason to deny the computer expert's assessment. He didn't waste any time getting down to the crux of the problem. "I tried to crack the password and the hard drive went into self-destruct mode."

"Amateur." Big laughed. "So I take it the drive is fried?"

"Don't know," Nick told him honestly. "The power plug was pulled out before the program reached the end of the countdown."

Bigelow nodded his head in approval. "Simple but direct. Quick thinking for a non-geek. There's hope for you yet."

Nick never took credit when it wasn't due. This time was no exception. "I wasn't the one who pulled the plug out of the socket."

Bigelow laughed to himself. "I should have known. So, what kind of a timeframe are we looking at. When do you need this by?"

Nick didn't beat about the bush, or couch his answer in niceties. "Yesterday."

This time the laugh was hearty. "Still always in a hurry, I see." Finishing his sandwich, Bigelow wiped his mouth, tossed the napkin onto his plate and leaned back in his chair. He studied the computer for several seconds before raising his eyes to his friend's. "So what's the story behind this?"

Nick filled him in, giving him all the information he had at the moment. Bigelow accepted it as his due. It had to do with respect for him as well as for his overall expertise.

"The computer tower belongs to a sheriff who was murdered sometime yesterday and then dumped in a shallow grave." For now, Nick kept the fact that Burris was one of three bodies, as well as the FBI's involvement in the case, to himself.

Bigelow regarded the tower thoughtfully before raising his eyes again. "And you think the reason he was murdered is on the computer?"

"Maybe," Nick allowed since he had no proof that he was right—although the hard drive attempting to self-destruct seemed like a dead giveaway. "Right now we're just looking into everything," Nick admitted to the other man.

"This sheriff have a name?" Bigelow asked.

"Most sheriffs do," Nick replied wryly. When his friend continued to look at him, one thick black eyebrow raised expectantly, Nick told him the man's name. "Peter Burris."

The response he got from Bigelow was not one he expected or was prepared for. "You're serious," Bigelow demanded in obvious disbelief. "Well, son of a gun, looks like Burris's sins finally caught up with him." The laugh had a hollow ring to it as he shook his head again. "How about that?"

"Back up, Big," Nick requested, trying to factor in this latest piece information he'd just been thrown. A new wave of anticipation telegraphed itself through his body. "You *know* Burris?"

"Wrong tense if he's dead," Bigelow pointed out. "But yeah, I knew *of* him," he said, emphasizing the difference. "Saw him a couple of times while he was still on the force, heard about him a lot more."

Nick wanted to be very clear on this. "Go on."

"Okay. From what I knew, Burris disappeared rather abruptly. The official story had it that he left for personal reasons, but the rumor was that there was some kind of scandal behind his now-you-see-him-now-you-don't act. He got the wrong people angry," Bigelow told him. "Heard he worked security for some kind of upscale nightclub here in Dallas after that. Then he left that to become the sheriff of Dogpatch, or some such story."

"Actually, he became a county sheriff, but I think you're referring to Vengeance," Nick corrected. "The name of the town is Vengeance." He was surprised at the prick of annoyance he felt to hear the place he lived being belittled. He'd thought himself indifferent to the town. Maybe he wasn't so indifferent to it after all. "It's a forty-mile drive from here."

"I'll put it on my list of places to see," Bigelow quipped. "Vengeance," he repeated, somewhat amused. "Sounds like a place Burris would go to. Heard he wasn't exactly a very forgiving man," he explained. And then Bigelow looked at the tower that Nick had brought in with him. This time he gave it a far more interested once-over. "So this was his, huh?"

Nick nodded. "I'd be really grateful for anything you can manage to pull off it."

"Grateful, hell," Bigelow mocked. "I get anything off this little beauty and you'll owe me your first-born."

"Not much chance of that," Nick assured the other man flatly.

Bigelow looked at him knowingly. "Still swearing off commitments, huh?"

"Let's just say I'm married to the job," Nick told him crisply.

"That'll get old eventually. Job can't keep you warm at night, or curl your toes when they need curling."

"Don't stay up nights worrying about my toes, Big. I'll manage." He nodded at the tower. "When do you think you can have something for me?"

Bigelow shook his head again. "Still as laidback as ever, I see." He regarded the tower. "It's not like I can work on this on the clock."

"Can't you pull some personal time?" Nick suggested. "I've got a hunch this is the key to Burris's murder." He looked at the other man. "I'll owe you one."

"You'll owe me twelve," Bigelow said, but it was obvious that his curiosity had definitely been aroused. "Okay, leave it with me," he instructed. "I'll give you a call if I find something."

Nick rose to his feet. "I need it sooner than later," he emphasized. He paused a second, then decided to give the tech expert another piece of information. Maybe it would motivate him. Bigelow always had a strong sense of competition. "The FBI's involved in this."

"The FBI?" Bigelow repeated incredulously. "Anything else you want to share? Like the name of some other alphabet-crazed federal bureau that's in on this, too?"

"No, as far as I know it's just the Vengeance police force and the FBI," Nick told his friend.

"FBI has its own lab techs," Bigelow pointed out. "Why bring it to me?"

The answer was simple—and one he knew would appeal to his friend. "Because you're the best, Big."

"More flattery. Cheap trick," Bigelow pointed out. And then he shrugged his thin shoulders. "Lucky for you, it works. Give me a few hours or so, I'll see what I can do." With that, Bigelow rose as well, tucking the tower under his arm.

He looked, Nick couldn't help thinking, like a kid who had just gotten what he wanted for Christmas and was about to take it apart to see what made it tick. He knew from the old days that Bigelow liked nothing better than to pit his intelligence against a computer and take the machine down.

* * *

Life Goes On.

It was a motto that John Abramowitz, the head dean of Darby College, had hanging on the wall behind his desk. His wife had needlepointed it for their first wedding anniversary. It was a simple truth that couldn't be disputed. No matter what happened, good or bad, life always went on.

And so it was at the college, even though their most celebrated professor, Melinda Grayson, had apparently been abducted.

Although, he thought nervously, as of yet, there had been no ransom demand made. Shouldn't there have been a demand by now?

As the head of the college, Abramowitz fully expected that the demand would be directed to him, since Melinda Grayson had no close family to speak of anywhere in the state.

All there was, if he remembered her application form correctly when she'd submitted her résumé to the college, was an ex-husband. Ex-husbands weren't known to step up with the proper ransom money when their ex-wives were kidnapped.

No, the note or the call regarding the amount of the ransom and where to drop it off would have come to him, and so far, there hadn't been any.

In the meantime, life had to go on. And so did Professor Grayson's classes. Someone would have to step in and temporarily take her place. The classes were all filled with students, all waiting to be taught something that would make the price of their tuition seem worthwhile, or at least bearable.

Fortunately, as if blessed with some futuristic insight, the professor had left behind lesson plans and very detailed notes for each of the upcoming classes in the semester ahead. Lesson plans and notes he intended to pass on to the assistants he was about to assign to take over her classes. The two assistants stood at attention, waiting for his direction.

"Sit down, please," Abramowitz requested, gesturing to the two chairs before his two-hundred-year-old hand-carved, hand-oiled desk. When they did, the dean got started. "As you might know, Dr. Grayson is currently missing—"

"Excuse me, Dean, but wasn't she kidnapped?" Ben Craig asked. "I thought I heard that she—"

"That is one school of thought," Abramowitz allowed, cutting the grad student off. His eyes swept over the lanky young man, and then Amanda Burns, the other graduate assistant he'd called into his office. "But until the school receives an official confirmation that she has indeed been kidnapped, the professor is just currently not on campus. Hopefully, that situation will change soon." He steepled his fingers together as he leaned back in his chair. "But, until she does return, she has classes that need to be helmed."

Dropping his hands back down, Abramowitz leaned forward over his desk, his small eyes looking at each student in turn, forming a silent bond with them—or so he assumed.

"Which is why I've asked you both to be here. I would like the two of you to split her classes between you and take them over."

"Take them over?" Amanda echoed, stunned and more than a little nervous about the very thought of having to step into the professor's shoes. "But we can't take her place."

"No one is asking you to take her place, Ms. Burns," Abramowitz pointed out patiently. "What the department needs is to have you and Mr. Craig just fill in for a little while," he instructed. "With any luck, it won't be for too long. You are both familiar with Dr. Grayson's work—"

"Familiar, yes," Craig agreed, interrupting. "But

those are really giant shoes you're asking us to fill, even temporarily." He began enumerating all the things that needed to be put into place. "We need time to prepare lesson plans for the classes, see what material needs to be covered—"

Having quickly worked up a full head of steam, Ben was forced to stop talking because the dean was holding up his hand.

"That's all been taken care of, Mr. Craig. It seems that Professor Grayson had all her lesson plans already written up for the entire semester, so all you two need to do is stick closely to it, teach what she had intended to teach, and everything will be fine." Abramowitz smiled broadly, as if what he'd just proposed were as simple as breathing.

The two graduate students, however, didn't seem that easily convinced.

"She had them all written out?" Amanda asked in disbelief. "Really?"

"Yes. Lucky, I know," the dean said, agreeing with what he thought both the students were thinking. "I found the lectures in her study after the FBI finally allowed me to have access to her home. They'd been left neatly on her desk, all labeled, in chronological order, with a separate sheet of notes tucked into each dated folder."

"Wow," Ben couldn't help murmuring under his breath, "talk about being anal."

The remark, audible enough for the dean to hear, earned him a rather annoyed, withering look. "Lucky for Darby College that the professor is such a stickler for detail," Abramowitz said, deliberately rephrasing Ben's assessment. He indicated the two stacks of papers on his desk. There was a preprinted sheet on top of each stack. "Now here are the classes, along with her notes. Sort it out between the two of you and be sure to stay on schedule so that when the professor finally returns, she'll be able to pick up just where you left off."

"You really think she's coming back, Dean?" Amanda asked him nervously.

"I most certainly do," Abramowitz assured her with alacrity.

In her short time at the college, the professor had swiftly earned near-celebrity status. That in turn had brought a great deal of attention to their little, heretofore unheard of college. The dean wouldn't allow himself to contemplate anything *less* than the woman's unharmed return. Getting her safe return was his ultimate goal and he was determined to reach it, no matter what it cost.

The phone rang, rousing Nick from a dead sleep. He had no recollection of laying down, but he must have because when he jolted into a sitting position, he realized that he had sprawled out on his sofa.

Damn, but his back hurt. He needed to invest in a new sofa, he thought grudgingly, clearing the cobwebs from his brain.

A beat later, he realized what had woken him up.

Focusing on the source of the ringing, Nick grabbed the landline receiver, put it against his ear and growled, "Jeffries," into the mouthpiece.

"You sitting down, Jeffries?"

It took him a second—because his brain was still struggling out of the haze that had surrounded it—but he managed to recognize the voice.

Bigelow.

The lab tech he'd gone out of his way to approach earlier today.

"In a manner of speaking," Nick mumbled, dragging a hand through his hair and trying to pull his thoughts together at the same time. Neither was a complete success.

"I finally cracked Burris's password and got into the computer," Bigelow announced with no small amount of triumph in his voice.

Nick might have been sleepy before, but he was wide awake now. "And?" he prodded. He knew that Bigelow liked his share of drama and, when there wasn't any, he had no problem with building it up himself.

"*And,* my friend, it seems that your town's dead sheriff was one hell of a busy little beaver while he was still alive. Burris was into all kinds of stuff—if what I just pulled off his computer was on the level." He paused for a moment, as if waiting for a drum roll. "—not the least of which was blackmail."

"Blackmail?" Nick echoed, stunned. "Who was he blackmailing? Were you able to get a name?" he asked.

"Oh, I got a name, all right," Bigelow assured him. "Seems our black-hearted sheriff was blackmailing a number of people, but I think you're really going to like his main target."

Nick waited for a second, but Bigelow was silent, drawing the moment out. "And that was?" he prodded. "C'mon, Big, it's the middle of the night. Don't make me beg."

"All right, all right, but just because we're friends. Peter Burris was blackmailing Senator John Merris."

Chapter 8

At this point in his life and career, Nick was confident that very few things could still surprise him.

What Chester Bigelow had just told him, however, definitely qualified as one of those few things.

"Are you there, Jeffries?" Bigelow asked when he received no response from the other end of the line. "Did you hear what I just said?"

"I heard you, Big," Nick answered. The case was officially messy now—if what Bigelow had just said was true. "Are you absolutely sure about this?"

Nick heard the man sigh impatiently. "I did what you said, I took some personal time and I've been working on recovering information from this damn hard drive since you brought it in. I haven't been to bed yet, so, yeah, I'm sure," Bigelow retorted waspishly. "I could email all this to you—and there's a hell of a lot of stuff—this guy documented *everything*—guess he wanted to make sure he didn't wind up being blackmailed himself." Bigelow paused, as if reconsidering what he'd just offered to do. "Tell you the truth, I'd rather not put it out there," the tech told him. "You never know who could hack into your system. How soon can you get over to my place?"

Nick looked at his watch again, trying to get his brain to engage and actually *see* the numbers. It was half past two—not that it affected his answer one way or another. He did a quick estimate involving traffic at this time of night and distance.

"I can be at the Dallas station in less than an hour."

"Don't go to the station. I'm at my house." Bigelow proceeded to rattle off his home address. "I'll be on the lookout for you. I take it you still drive with a lead foot. One hour, huh?"

With the phone receiver nestled against his

shoulder and neck, Nick was already shrugging into the shirt he'd absently discarded last night. He was still wearing the jeans he'd changed into when he came home.

"Give or take."

"I'd rather give," Bigelow told him. "Okay, see you soon." And with that, the line went dead as the call was abruptly terminated.

Nick staggered into his master bathroom, threw some water onto his face and went looking for his shoes, which weren't where they were supposed to be.

The search for his shoes made him think of Suzy Burris and the high heels she'd had on—and how sexy her legs had looked to him.

Pushing aside his intense, immediate reaction to her image—damn, he was going to have to really police himself more stringently—he focused on the problem of her late husband.

Had she really been oblivious to what Big had just uncovered? Had Burris managed to keep all this from her, or was she actually his silent partner, taking part in his blackmail scheme?

Nick vacillated between feeling protective of her and angry for being duped by the woman.

She hadn't said anything about *any* of this to

him yesterday. Was she just being secretive, or had she *really* been in the dark about this?

And just what was this information going to do to the investigation—besides blowing it sky high?

It couldn't be just a weird coincidence that the Senator had been killed, too.

Or could it?

Had Burris conducted the blackmailing on his own, or was he an instrument for yet another, unknown party? Had that "unknown party" been the one to have killed Burris? Why?

And what did the third victim, David Reed, have to do with any of this?

Damn, Nick thought in exasperation as he hurried out of his house and into his car, he had far more questions than he had answers. Certainly a hell of a lot more questions now than he'd had before.

This investigation was *not* going well.

Nick turned up the music. It was going to be a long drive.

She'd been right. Even with Lori there to take over caring for Andy during the night, she hadn't been able to sleep more than a few minutes at a time. And even those minutes were comprised of sleep that could only be termed as fitful.

Consequently, Suzy was up and sitting in the kitchen, nursing a cup of coffee when she heard the doorbell. Glancing at the watch that was only off her wrist when she showered, Suzy frowned.

She wasn't expecting anyone. Who could be on her doorstep at seven in the morning?

It had to be a reporter, she decided. Who else would be so insensitive as to bother her at this hour, especially just after her husband had been murdered?

By the time she reached the front door and yanked it open, Suzy had worked up a full head of steam. She was more than ready to give the person standing on the other side of the door a piece of her mind.

The hot words hovering on her lips died when she saw a rather rumpled-looking Nick Jeffries on her doorstep.

What was he doing here at this hour? She couldn't tell by his expression if it was good news or bad news that he was bringing her. Suzy braced herself for the worst, just in case.

"Detective, are you all right?" she asked,

quickly looking him up and down. She couldn't come to a conclusion—other than he looked tired.

Welcome to the club, she thought.

"Did you know?" Nick asked sharply.

It wasn't quite an accusation, but there would be no room for forgiveness if she'd knowingly lied to him and he made that clear by the tone of voice he used.

Suzy stared at him. She hadn't the slightest idea what the detective was talking about—but his tone made her uneasy.

"Did I know what?"

Nick strode past her into the house, pushing the door closed behind him. He was in no mood for her to play innocent.

"Did you know that your husband was black-mailing a number of people, including Senator Merris?" He swung around to look at her. "One of the two other murder victims found near your husband's grave."

Suzy turned pale.

This couldn't be happening.

Just when she thought that it couldn't get any worse, it did. Who *was* this man she'd married? When had he managed to do all this? It didn't seem possible. Could she have been so blind to this darker side of his?

"He was *what?*" she cried, staring dumbfounded, at Nick.

"Blackmailing Senator Merris." No one could fake that pale color that had just come over her face, he thought. His anger vanished as quickly as it had materialized. She wasn't in on this with the sheriff. She looked too stunned and upset. Compassion made a comeback, stirring his gut.

"You didn't know, did you?"

The detective's voice became a distant buzzing in her head. None of the words registered as Suzy somehow managed to make her way to the sofa. Clutching the armrest, she sank down.

Actually, her knees just gave way a second before she reached the sofa. But rather than go down on the floor, she'd been caught. Held.

Suzy was vaguely aware of arms closing around her. Aware of a presence beside her, a person whose touch was exceedingly gentle. It was understood that she would shatter if any sort of actual physical pressure, no matter how well meaning, was applied to her limbs.

And although she'd always thought of herself as

tough and made of sterner stuff, at this moment, she wasn't all that sure that she *wouldn't* shatter.

She heard the command "Breathe!" uttered near her ear and did as she was told, drawing in air, and then slowly releasing it again.

Once, twice—by the third lungful of air, Suzy had begun to come around, to be able to focus again.

She blinked a number of times, and then looked to see that the detective whose revelation had just torpedoed her world for a second time in two days was the one sitting beside her on the sofa, his arm protectively around her shoulders.

He'd created a haven for her.

There *was* no such thing, she told herself bitterly the next second, feeling numb and hopelessly betrayed at the same time.

"I'm okay," she told Nick.

But when she tried to get up, she found that the detective was firmly holding her in place, his hands on her shoulders.

"Sit for a little longer," he told her. It wasn't a suggestion. "I don't think you want me picking you up from the floor."

He was talking about fainting. Just like she'd

done the day before. Suzy had no intentions of embarrassing herself twice in two days.

"I wasn't going to faint," she protested.

"Whatever you say," Nick allowed philosophically. Now that he realized she'd had no part in Burris's dark actions, he was feeling bad for having detonated this newest bombshell on her like this. "But humor me for a couple of minutes."

Suzy shrugged carelessly, remaining where she was. Not so much because she was going along with the detective's veiled order, but because what he'd just said had all but paralyzed her, or at least had frozen her in place.

Where did she begin to try to untangle all she'd been hit with?

Feeling utterly helpless, she looked at Nick and clutched at a straw. "Are you sure? About Peter blackmailing people? And what did he have on them? How could he be blackmailing someone? Why would he do such a terrible thing?"

Suzy suddenly covered her mouth with her hands, as if she was attempting to physically hold back the questions until she could organize them so that they made more sense.

"God, you must think I'm a total idiot not to know about any of this." Her eyes shifted to his.

"But I didn't. I swear I didn't. When Peter didn't talk to me, I didn't realize that there was this much he wasn't talking about."

Suzy blew out a long breath, feeling completely overwhelmed.

"A lot of smart people get fooled by people they trust," Nick told her gently. "Did you ever notice the sheriff spending lavish amounts of money, buying large-ticket items he wouldn't have been able to afford on a sheriff's salary?"

She shook her head. *That* she would have noticed. "No, nothing. No fancy clothes, no vacations, no expensive cars, nothing," she insisted. "You can search the house if you like." She dragged her hand through her hair. It hung loose, like a blond storm, about her shoulders.

This all sounded like something out of a movie, not her life. "Everyone seemed to like him," she told Nick helplessly. She'd already told him that, she realized, but it was the only thing she could think of to offer as a defense.

And then, overwhelmed, she shook her head. "It's like he had this whole other life that I didn't know about." It would take her a while to wrap her head around this. To believe that Peter had done all these things. "So do you think that this—this blackmailing that Peter was doing—was what had gotten him killed?"

At the moment, that was the million-dollar question, Nick thought.

Out loud, he said honestly, "I don't know. Especially since the main person he appeared to be blackmailing was Senator Merris and like I said, Merris was buried in the grave near your husband."

"Blackmail," she repeated incredulously. It was so hard to believe. "And here I thought that Peter's affairs were the most sordid thing he was guilty of. I guess that really shows me," she laughed harshly, a trace of bitterness hovering around her words.

She suddenly looked very fragile to him. Moreover, Nick was actually feeling her pain and all the insecurity the situation generated. She was the kind of person, he sensed, who felt responsible for her husband's shortcomings. But it wasn't her fault.

"What your husband did has nothing to do with you," Nick told her firmly. Placing the crook of his finger beneath her chin, he raised her head so that her eyes met his. "The only people we are responsible for in this life are ourselves. Sometimes a spouse does evil things that you might feel reflect badly on the person they're married to but the real truth of it is, it just reflects badly on them.

Most of the time, their spouse has nothing to do with their bad behavior. They don't even know anything about it."

She looked at him for a long moment. And then she understood. Nick had gone through this himself.

"You sound like you know about that firsthand." And just like that, the tables turned. Sympathy rose like a solid wall when she saw him shrug at her words. "Are you married, Nick?"

He thought of the wife he'd once loved. And of the woman who had ultimately betrayed his trust. It seemed like a hundred years ago now.

"No," he responded, his voice distant.

She wasn't ready to let this go just yet. Nothing made her forget about her own situation faster than someone else in need of comfort. "But you were?"

He could have easily said that his marital state had no bearing on the case. But instead, he heard himself answering her question. Maybe it was because he felt he owed it to her because he'd pried into her life.

"Once."

Suzy made assumptions from the look she saw in his eyes. "And she kept secrets from you?"

"As far as I know, there was only one thing she

kept from me." Maybe there had been more than one, he didn't know. He hadn't stuck around to find out. It was the one that had ended their marriage.

Suzy backed off. She didn't want to cause him any undue pain, especially since she now knew what that felt like. "I'm sorry, I have no right to pick at your wounds."

The denial came quickly and automatically. "It's not a wound. Besides, it happened a long time ago." He supposed, if he were really over it, he could talk about it without any residual pain.

He braced himself anyway.

"She was pregnant and she didn't tell me." He looked away, not really seeing anything. It went along with distancing himself from the words he said. "She just decided not to be."

"Oh."

The full impact of his words hit her and Suzy knew that what she saw in his eyes, despite his detached, distant voice, was raw pain. Rather than offer any platitudes or say something that would just sound inane, she put her hand over his, silently offering him her condolences as well as a mute offer of support and comfort should he want either.

When she looked back on this later, Suzy realized that this was the moment when they ceased to be just polite strangers on opposite ends of a murder investigation.

This was the moment that they bonded.

Clearing his throat—as if that would somehow also clear the air and clear away the words that had just been uttered—Nick said, "I think your husband might have been blackmailing the senator for money. Did your husband handle the banking?"

"No, actually, I did. I'm a certified public accountant," she explained. "I've been on maternity leave these last couple of months," she added, "but until Andy was born, I worked full-time for a restaurant chain and took care of all our monthly bills as well. Peter hated being bothered with all those details," she told him matter-of-factly. She realized now that he was just too busy with all the other things he was into. "So I just took over."

"And you have a joint savings account?" Nick asked her.

"Yes—and a joint checking account, too."

"Which bank?" he asked.

"First National Bank of Vengeance," she told him. An ironic smile curved her lips. "I always said that it needed a better name."

He made no comment on that. In his opinion, the whole *town* needed a better name than the one they had accepted. But that was neither here nor there right now.

"Would you mind coming to the bank with me?" he asked.

"No problem," she answered. Lori would stay here with the baby, so she was free to take off and try to possibly help undo a little of the damage that her husband had been responsible for. "Mind if I ask what you're hoping to accomplish?"

"I want to find out if Peter had another account, under his own name." It wasn't the smartest thing in the whole world to have a secret account in the same bank where your joint accounts with your wife are, but then the man in question didn't strike him as being the sharpest knife in the drawer— even if he were the *only* knife in the drawer.

She might as well get everything over with at once, find out just how black the picture was, she decided. "All right."

He didn't want her to think he was rushing her. The bank still had over an hour and a half before it would open its doors.

Nick looked at his watch and did a quick calculation. "Why don't I give you a couple of hours to have breakfast and get ready? I can come back at around nine and we can go to the bank then?"

"Do you have someplace that you have to be for the next two hours?" she asked. She had a feeling she already knew the answer to that, but waited for him to tell her anyway.

"No, but—"

"Then stay here," she urged. "Once I get ready, I can make us all some breakfast—unless you already ate—"

He'd come straight from Big's Dallas apartment to her door, stopping only for some coffee in order to fuel up and keep going—preferably awake.

"No, I haven't had breakfast yet," he answered.

Her smile lit up her face he noted, almost against his will.

"Okay, give me about ten minutes to get showered and dressed, and then I'll see what I can come up with for breakfast."

"Ten minutes?" he echoed incredulously, staring at her. "Did you just say that you could get ready in ten minutes?"

"Yes." Suzy couldn't see why he would look so surprised at that. "Why?"

He laughed shortly. "Nothing, except I've never known a woman yet who could get ready for anything in under an hour. Certainly not in ten minutes," Nick scoffed.

She smiled at him, taking a tiny personal moment out of what felt like it had the makings of an absolutely awful day if the first hour was any indication.

"That's because you've never known me before, Detective," she assured him. And then she grew serious. "If you suddenly feel as if you're starving, feel free to help yourself to anything in the refrigerator while you wait," she tossed over her shoulder.

He stood where she'd left him, watching Suzy hurry up the stairs. The sway of her hips seemed almost rhythmic to him.

No, he thought, *I've never known someone quite like you before.*

Nick wasn't aware he was smiling until he caught a glimpse of his reflection in the window as he passed by.

Chapter 9

Nick wasn't one of those people who had a favorite restaurant or even a favorite dish. Ever since his divorce, he was more apt to eat whenever he was hungry rather than at a given time. He adhered to structure in his professional life. His private life, however, was a different matter. It was entirely flexible.

So when he sat at the kitchen table and the sheriff's widow placed a Spanish omelet before him, urging him to "dig in," he was surprised to discover his appetite kicking in. His taste buds came to life as a rather spicy, tantalizing taste registered when he took his first bite of the omelet.

Nick looked down at his plate as if he'd just had a whole new taste experience. That was as surprising to him as his unexpected attraction to Suzy Burris had been.

"What's in this?" he asked.

"Is it too spicy for you?" she guessed, concerned. Lori had opted to take her breakfast later and was tending to Andy so it was just the two of them in the kitchen. Suzy slid into the chair directly opposite her unexpected guest.

"No, it's not *too* spicy," he allowed, "but it is definitely spicy. And really good," he told her belatedly. He wasn't much on giving compliments so it felt rather awkward on his tongue. But he thought it only right to let her know that he was enjoying what she'd just made. "What's in this?" he asked again.

She merely smiled, pleased that she'd actually made something that the detective enjoyed eating. It had been a long time since she'd gotten positive feedback of any kind, and that included on her cooking. The only way she knew if Peter liked something or not was that if he didn't like what she'd made, he'd leave it on his plate.

"Oh, a little bit of everything. That's what's so neat about this recipe, you can use practically anything you have on hand that's edible. This time around I used ham, cheese, mushrooms, eggs, of course and one tiny, diced-up jalapeño. That's the spicy part," she told him with a grin, then nodded over toward the stove. "There's more if you're still hungry."

"Maybe later," he told her. "Right now, I have a feeling that if I get too full, I'm just going to get sleepy, and there's no time for that. The clock's ticking on this," he said with emphasis.

That had a very ominous sound to it, Suzy thought. "What aren't you telling me?" she asked.

He'd made a quick pit stop to his desk at the station and had run into one of the FBI special agents who had been assigned to the triple homicide. The special agent had yet to figure out how, but he felt that the murders were somehow tied in to Dr. Grayson's disappearance. And the longer the woman remained missing, the less likely, in the special agent's opinion, that she would be found still alive.

The information had been shared with him in confidence. It wasn't for the general public's knowledge and despite the fact that Suzy Burris wasn't exactly part of the general public in this case, he still felt that he couldn't share it with the sheriff's widow, at least not at this time.

"Nothing that I know of," he told her, his voice devoid of any emotion. "But the sooner we find out who killed your husband and the others, the sooner we can get him—or her—off the street, and that can only be a good thing."

Suzy read between the lines. This wasn't over yet. "So you think this person might kill again?"

She was watching him so intently, he could almost *feel* her eyes on him. Nick realized that it took effort for him not to react. He kept his focus on the case and *not* on the fact that something about Suzy Burris was definitely getting to him.

It had to be the vulnerability angle, he told himself the next moment. The fact that she was a petite, slender blonde with sky-blue eyes was neither here nor there. He'd interacted with his share of attractive women and hadn't experienced any feelings one way or another.

Yet feelings—dormant feelings—kept insisting on coming into play here.

"If he's a serial killer, yes," he told her, controlling his voice. "If this was done strictly for revenge or some other specific reason known only to the killer, then no. But we're not at the point when we can be sure of that one way or another," he told her. "And since that's the case right now, I'd much rather err on the side of caution than be too laid-back and face possible consequences because of that."

Suzy had eaten rather quickly while the detective talked and now rose again, taking her plate to the sink. "All right," she announced, crossing back to the table and him, "I'm all yours."

He had no idea why that simple sentence hit him the way it did, or why, for just a fraction of a moment, his imagination went to places that had nothing to do with his investigation and everything to do with him as a man—and her as a woman.

The glimmer of sexual attraction he had become aware of yesterday seemed to have been simmering on some backburner ever since, and now kept insisting on springing forward, grabbing at and demanding his full, undivided attention.

He had no time for that now—or ever, really. He'd tried marriage once, found that it was an ill fit for him and had made his peace with that years ago as the ink dried on his signature on the divorce papers.

Or so he had believed until he'd encountered

Suzy Burris. Now he seemed to have this—for lack of a better term—pervasive restlessness haunting him. It was hiding in the corners of his focus, popping out at will, unannounced and un-expected, to throw him off balance.

"Detective?" she said, looking at him curiously. When he still made no response, Suzy came closer, tilting her head as she looked at him and tried again. She used his first name this time. "Nick?"

"Sorry, just thinking," Nick said, brushing off the question he saw in her eyes.

He felt fairly confident that the woman would assume that he was thinking about the case—and not her. Although right now, she very well could figure into this scenario prominently. He needed to find out if there was anything that Suzy Burris *did* know about her husband's dealings.

"When you met your husband, was he already the county sheriff?"

When she met her husband, she couldn't help thinking, he seemed like a completely different man. Which had been the real Peter Burris? The one from those days, or the one who'd died ap-proximately three days ago?

She shook her head in response to the ques-tion. "No, he was working a security detail at a nightclub in Dallas." She recalled that Nick had mentioned the DPD yesterday. "He never said anything about having worked as a police detective anywhere."

Well, if he had amassed the kind of record that Burris had, he wouldn't have readily admitted his connection to the police force to anyone, either. Nick thought.

"So when your husband stopped working security detail, was that your idea, or his?" Nick asked.

Your husband.

What a joke, she thought. Husbands were supposed to share things with their wives. Right now, she couldn't think of Peter as anything but a stranger.

"His," she told Nick, then admitted, "it happened rather suddenly, actually. He came home one night and said he had this big surprise—that we were leaving Dallas because he'd scored a plum position—he was going to be a county sheriff."

At the time, she welcomed a change of scenery. Things had already been getting stale and going badly between them. A change of venue could be the shot in the arm they both needed, she'd reasoned.

But she'd been wrong.

"I thought we'd be moving to Houston or San Antonio— When he said we were getting a house in Vengeance, I thought he was kidding. I'd never *heard* of Vengeance until then," she confessed.

He nodded understandingly. "It's not exactly on the list of the country's ten major cities. Did you try to talk him out of it?" he asked.

She shook her head. "I didn't have the heart. He seemed too excited about getting the job. And, to be honest, I wasn't exactly happy about where I was working, so leaving wasn't really a hardship."

From where he was sitting, Nick thought, Burris had it all—a beautiful wife and a promising career. What had he done that caused it to all go south on him?

"Did your husband happen to say what brought about this sudden change in careers?"

This keeping things to himself had its roots in those early days, she realized now. "No, only that he thought his luck was finally changing."

"So you didn't know that he was a dirty cop," he pressed, watching her face for some telltale sign that would indicate she was lying to him, or that she'd known that her husband was corrupt.

Suzy grew very still. He saw all the joy that had

been there only moments ago while they were casually talking, abruptly disappear.

"What did he do?" she asked in a voice that was completely drained of any emotion, any feeling. A voice that belonged to a shell-shocked woman.

Ordinarily, Nick didn't pull punches, but he found himself weighing his words, searching around for euphemisms.

"I think he might have been doing favors for people who were in a position to show him their gratitude. Apparently, some of the cases he handled while on the force had to be dismissed when crucial evidence would mysteriously go missing.

"When your husband moved on to work security at that nightclub he somehow got wind of the fact that Senator Merris had being siphoning off millions from his oil company, funneling it to his election campaign. He used the money to get himself elected, while other people wound up going bankrupt. Your husband found out and used this to blackmail the senator. Merris pulled some strings, got the old sheriff to suddenly retire and gave your husband the county sheriff's job in exchange for his silence."

He paused for a moment, letting his words sink in, and then told her, "From some of the things your husband had on his computer, I'd say that the blackmail didn't exactly end there."

She felt overwhelmed and struggled to find a way to rise above this quicksand of demoralizing corruption.

She asked the same question she'd put to him earlier. "And this is what ultimately got Peter killed?" It was all very hard to fathom—but she had this sinking feeling that, if anything, the detective with the kind eyes was now trying to downplay all this for her benefit.

"That would be the logical assumption—except that the senator was found dead, too," he reminded her, and went on to mention again the fly in the ointment. "And I still don't know how David Reed figures into this."

It would take her a long, long time to put this all behind her. She wasn't in love with Peter, but she'd still believed that, at bottom, he was a good man. Now that belief just mocked her and made her feel incapable of judging a person's true character. Any guilt over her lack of grief was wiped out by the fact that, apparently, she'd been married to someone she didn't know. Someone she *never* got to know.

"I *knew* there were things that Peter was keeping from me, but I had no idea it was something like *this*. I just thought his secrecy had to do with other women he was seeing." Had there been signs that she'd missed? Or had she just been oblivious to it all because she'd wanted to be?

"He had his share of those, too," Nick told her.

He would have rather not said anything about it, but he knew the media. Once they started digging, they would splash it across the TV screen. He wanted Suzy to be prepared for the firestorm rather than be taken by surprise.

She struggled not to loathe the man she'd married—the man she'd *thought* she'd married.

"It doesn't make any sense," Suzy cried, anger flaring in her voice. "Why would Peter want to have a baby with me when he had all this going on at the same time? Why would he want to stay married to me at all?"

Nick could easily see why the sheriff would have wanted to stay married to Suzy. Why *any* man would have wanted to be married to her. He had trouble seeing why Burris had so wantonly thrown it all away.

Nick approached her question from another, logical angle. "Maybe he wanted to have his cake and eat it, too. Being married with a family adds to the image of an upstanding lawman. You told me that most people liked the sheriff—"

She shrugged. "Maybe I was wrong about that, too. Seems I was wrong about everything else," she said disparagingly.

She was standing, facing the kitchen window, no longer able to make eye contact. Afraid that if she saw pity in Nick's eyes, she'd break down and cry. That was the last thing she wanted to do, fall apart in front of someone else.

Nick sensed what she was going through, what recriminations she was heaping on herself in the privacy of her own mind. He'd been there himself, except that his wife hadn't been in a place of public trust. But she'd turned out to be a fraud and a cheat in her own way just the same. He had felt just as empty, just as devastated, just as betrayed as he knew Suzy was feeling right now.

He came up behind her. Placing his hands on her shoulders, he turned Suzy slowly around to face him. "None of this is your fault."

So he'd already said before. She kept her eyes down, not wanting to meet his. Her voice was thick with emotion and tears she refused to shed.

"Maybe not, but being blind is. How could all this have been going on and I didn't have a clue?"

He'd asked himself that same question at the time. "Don't forget, the sheriff was undoubtedly very good. He managed to fool a lot of other people besides you—otherwise, he would have been up on charges and in prison a long time ago," Nick told her.

She supposed he had a point, but that didn't help her now.

"If I'd only known, I wouldn't have agreed to have Andy." Anguish filled her eyes. "How am I going to be able to tell my son, when he starts asking questions about where his father is, that his father was murdered because all the lying and cheating he'd done had finally caught up with him?"

Rather than answer her question, Nick asked her one of his own. It was short and to the point. "How do you feel about Andy?"

"Well, I love him, of course." That wasn't the issue. "He means everything to me, but—"

Nick stopped her before she could continue. She'd already said the relevant part.

"Then, don't you see, that's all that matters. You love him and you'll be there for him. He's your son and part of you. And in the end, having him will help *you* get through this."

Suzy pressed her lips together. He'd undone her with his kindness. Her emotions spilled out.

Nick saw the lone tear trickling down her cheek. The sight of it felt like a one-two punch straight to his gut. Holding himself in check, he took a breath, and then he took his thumb and very gently, wiped the tear away.

Suzy let out a very shaky breath. "You're very insightful for a police detective," she told him in a voice that was only slightly above a whisper. She was acutely aware of his closeness, his gentleness. Aware and finding herself getting incredibly warmed by it.

Maybe *too* warmed.

"It's my sensitivity training," Nick quipped, trying to be flippant, doing his damndest not to get reeled in any further by eyes the color of cornflowers in the spring or lips that he had a great deal of difficulty ignoring.

He'd brushed away her tear with his thumb and had been struck by how soft her skin felt. At the same moment, the realization of just how very long it had been since he had kissed a woman had hit him. Not just that, but also how very long it had been since he had *wanted* to kiss a woman.

And then, just like that, he was no longer thinking about how long it had been because the answer to that was not long at all. He was feeling it and he was doing it. Doing both.

Wanting and kissing.

Cupping Suzy's cheek with the palm of his hand, he'd lowered his mouth to hers.

Suzy remained very, very still, her eyes wide open and watching him. Afraid to move, afraid to take a breath, afraid that if she did either, she would break whatever spell had brought this moment about and make him back away.

When his lips touched hers, she felt the heart that had been, just a second ago, hammering double time all but sigh with pleasure.

The next second, as she leaned forward *into* the kiss, Suzy felt her pulse accelerate the way it used to when she was jogging and nearing the end of her run.

Except that this was far more exhilarating.

And almost as rewarding.

Still cupping her cheek, Nick took his other hand and framed her face, deepening the kiss he still couldn't bring himself to believe was happening.

Kissing her was definitely having its side effects. He could *swear* he was feeling somewhat lightheaded and, at the same time, incredibly and almost wildly exhilarated.

Damn it, Jeffries, get a grip! This has no place here! his brain was all but screaming at him, years of discipline warring with very strong, very basic needs and desires.

With a huge surge of regret thundering through his system, Nick pulled back. His hands were on her shoulders again as much to steady himself as to steady her.

How did he make this huge transgression right?

"I'm sorry," Nick began and was able to get no further.

He got no further because he couldn't. Couldn't form a single other word. This time, with her arms firmly linked around the back of his neck, *she* was kissing *him*.

When he'd pulled back, creating that chasmlike space between them, Suzy had looked up at him with dazed confusion, trying to process what he was saying to her and what she felt had to be his feelings behind his words. But then, instead of listening to anything further, instead of hearing something she might not want to hear, Suzy had launched herself back at him and had resumed the delicious, abruptly interrupted, kiss.

Because, at that particular moment, when Nick had kissed her without warning, she had realized that for the first time in close to a year, she felt alive.

More than that, she felt like a living, breathing *woman,* something that she hadn't felt like in the last year of what she now knew had been only a sham of a marriage.

This was what she'd wanted to feel when she was with Peter, but she hadn't—and now that she looked back, she realized that it had turned out for the best, though of course she'd never wanted him to die. Her love had been a lie, since he was a lie. Everything about Peter had been a lie. Had she truly loved him, it would have made things that much worse for her.

This kiss had been, Suzy suspected, an accident on Nick's part, a moment fueled by a temporary weakness. Whatever the reason behind it, she didn't care. Right now, all she cared about was the effect. She wanted to savor this sensation, this feeling before it was gone out of her life for good.

In a strange, roundabout way, she caught herself thinking before all thinking stopped, Peter was responsible for making this happen. It was the only decent thing he'd done for her in a long time, she thought, other than giving her Andy.

Chapter 10

Nick discovered, much to his surprise, that it was harder pulling away the second time around—because this kiss was even more enjoyable and arousing than the first kiss.

Somehow, he managed to draw away from the woman who'd stirred him to the point that he found himself ditching his principles, his training and his natural tendency to be cautious.

Had there been no investigation, no case that could possibly involve Suzy directly or indirectly, he would have been free to go with his instincts—

instincts he had been so very sure that he'd sealed away and left behind him years ago.

But then, had there been no investigation, their paths, his and Suzy's, most likely wouldn't have crossed. And even if they had, there would have still been a problem. At that point—if there'd been no murder—she would have been a married woman, he reminded himself.

It seemed that no matter how he sliced it, this— whatever *this* actually was—was just *not* supposed to be happening between them.

And yet, there was no denying that something was definitely happening between them.

It took Nick more than a couple of seconds to get his bearings—and that, too, surprised him. Until now, he'd always been able to land on his feet no matter *where* he fell from.

"I'm sorry, that shouldn't have happened," he apologized, taking the full blame for both occurrences. "It's just that you looked so upset and I wanted to help somehow."

Nick suppressed an exasperated sigh. That hadn't come out right. Words, whether verbal or written, had never been his long suit. He'd always been better at doing, at acting rather than talking. Now was no exception.

Despite everything that was going on, Suzy couldn't help but smile at him. This tall, powerful-looking police detective was stumbling around like a newborn colt trying to stand up on his unsteady legs.

"Actually, you did help," she responded. "It's been a long time since I've felt—anything."

Suzy left it at that, a vague statement he could interpret any way he wanted to. To say more now would only scare both of them off and she had no idea if what she was feeling was born of gratitude—or something else.

"Maybe I'd better come back later—tomorrow," Nick suggested, wanting to give her some time to reassess the situation—wanting to give himself some time, as well.

As far as he was concerned, this was nothing short of conduct unbecoming in his case and no matter how attractive he found the woman, that wasn't supposed to have any bearing on his behavior. He wasn't supposed to be acting on impulses even if his intentions had been honorable to begin with—or so he'd told himself.

"No, please." Suzy caught his sleeve, holding on to it far more firmly than he would have thought her capable of doing. "I want to help you with this investigation. I *need* to help," she emphasized. "The Peter Burris I knew wasn't a monster, but if what you're telling me is true, he was far from being the honest man he pretended to be and he did things that I will always be ashamed of—"

Nick didn't want her dwelling on that. "I told you, it's not your fault," he said firmly. "*None* of this is your fault."

"Then let me help," she requested simply.

He saw the need in her eyes and relented. Not to would have been cruel.

"All right, I could use another set of eyes as well as hands," he allowed. "And you'll probably make much less of a mess than I would—although," he warned her, "this is going to have to be a thorough search."

She wasn't going to hide. If there was something damning hidden here, it had to come out. And if there wasn't, then maybe the picture wasn't as black as Nick had painted it. Either way, she wanted the truth.

Suzy nodded. "I understand."

They spent the next several hours going over the three-bedroom home with a fine-tooth comb, emptying closets, clearing drawers, climbing up ladders and examining places that were normally inaccessible to anything but dust accumulation, such as the tops of kitchen cabinets. The search took twice as long as initially projected because they painstakingly disassembled then reassembled each room.

And for their trouble, they found a few things that Suzy had long thought lost. As far as discovering why Peter Burris had been murdered, along with the man who'd been his mark, or why there'd been a third victim thrown into those shallow graves, they got no further in their investigation.

Somewhat drained by the search and the subsequent disappointment, Nick suggested they take a break. They'd just finished going over the master bedroom and, crossing into the hallway, they sank down onto the floor, their backs resting against the wall.

Seeing her sister and the detective looking so weary, Lori must have taken pity on them. After putting Andy down for a nap, Suzy's sister hurried downstairs and within minutes returned to present each of them with a tall, frosty glass of pink lemonade.

Suzy took hers with both hands and first applied it to her forehead and cheek, absorbing the coolness with an appreciative sigh.

"You're a saint," Suzy told her. Lori had placed a straw into hers, just the way she preferred it. It had the effect of taking her back to the early days of her childhood, when life was far less complicated and demanding.

Before she became aware that her family unit was far from idyllic.

"That's not how she felt when we were growing up," Lori confided to Nick as she handed him his glass.

"You needed a lot of work back then," Suzy deadpanned. "But you let me guide you and you turned out really well."

"Guide me, ha!" Lori declared with a pseudo-haughty laugh. "I 'turned out really well' *despite* your so called guidance, dear sister, not because of it," she concluded with a triumphant note.

Nick had no idea if this was headed for a confrontation, or if it was some battle solely based on habitual banter, so he decided to divert the conversation into a different direction.

"This really hit the spot," he told Lori, holding up his glass after downing half the contents in one long gulp. He hadn't realized that he was *that* thirsty until Lori had handed him his lemon-ade. "Thanks."

Without turning around, Lori waved her hand over her head as a sign that she'd heard him and appreciated his comment. "My pleasure, Detective," she said just as she disappeared around the corner.

"So, is that every place?" Nick asked Suzy once he was alone with her again.

She nodded. They'd been through every room, including the nursery and all the bathrooms. "There's just Peter's car left—"

That, he thought, turned out to be another dead end. "I already had a crew go over that. They didn't find anything except that the late sheriff seemed to have a thing for chewing gum. There were a lot of discarded gum wrappers on the floor, both in the front *and* the back. Maybe he was going for a record in most accumulated gum wrappers."

She laughed shortly. "Peter tends—tended," she amended abruptly, correcting herself as she wondered how long it was going to take for her to get used to the idea that Peter was no longer among the living, "to chew gum when he was tense."

"Whatever he was doing that was making him tense, it was recent," Nick judged. "The wrappers hadn't gotten dried out from the sun shining into the vehicle," he told her. Finished with his lemonade, Nick wanted to get back to work. He rose to his feet then extended his hand to her to help her up.

Ordinarily, she would have ignored the silent offer of help and just gotten up on her own, but there was something about this man, something that made her trust him despite the way she had gotten burned in her marriage. Something that made her *want* his help. To welcome his touch.

So, placing her hand in his, she allowed Nick to help pull her up.

Taking in and releasing a long, cleansing breath, she looked up at him and asked, "Now what?"

Nick found he had to tear his eyes away from the way Suzy's chest rose and fell as she drew in that deeper breath.

That was *not* going to help him keep a clear head here, he upbraided himself silently.

Damn it, he *knew* better.

"I think I'd like to go over the sheriff's office one more time, see if we maybe we might have missed something."

She cocked her head, trying to keep things straight. "You mean Peter's office in town?"

"No, here," he corrected. "The FBI guys are

taking your husband's office in town apart piece by piece—most likely not making any points with the new, interim sheriff," he guessed. "They would have called if something had turned up."

She nodded. "All right, you go ahead." Suzy felt her stomach pinch her and she glanced at her watch. "It's getting late." As she talked, she started to lead the way downstairs. "I should start getting dinner ready." Stopping midway down, Suzy looked at him over her shoulder. "Would you like to stay? For dinner, I mean?" she clarified in case he thought she meant anything else.

Distance, you need to keep your distance. "I shouldn't—" Nick began.

"You have to eat, Nick," she insisted. She wanted him to understand that there was no need to reject her hospitality because of what had happened between them earlier. "And I promise to let you do it in peace."

There was a hint of an ironic smile curving Nick's lips. "You're not the one I'm concerned about," he told her.

Suzy stopped at the bottom of the stairs and turned around to look at him again. Amusement had crept into her eyes. "Oh?"

"Yeah, 'oh,'" was all he allowed himself to say by way of a comment on her reaction.

The truth was he didn't trust himself. It was almost as if, when he hadn't been paying attention, he'd undergone a breakdown in self-discipline.

But no matter how it came about, that would end as of this moment. Once was a fluke, not right but forgivable. Twice was the beginning of a pattern—and the end of his career as an impartial officer of law enforcement.

"So, three plates for dinner?" she asked, silently telling him that her sister would be joining them and that Lori would serve as their insurance policy that nothing remotely compromising would happen if he decided to stay for dinner.

She was a good cook and the prospect of heating up a frozen dinner or bringing something home from one of the takeout restaurants in his neighborhood didn't sound nearly as appealing, so after what amounted to an incredibly short internal debate, he nodded, accepting her invitation.

"Three," he echoed, then flashed what came across as a tight smile. "Thanks."

Suzy caught herself grinning in response. She was really pleased the detective was staying.

Maybe it was wrong of her, but she was beginning to see the light at the end of the tunnel and because of that light, she knew she would get through this ordeal intact.

And it was in large part due to the detective.

"Good—and don't mention it," she added as an afterthought.

They parted there, at the bottom of the stairs, each going their own way. She went to the kitchen while he went to give the sheriff's already carefully examined home office one last once-over.

He'd just walked into the center of the room when his cellphone rang. Nick had it out and against his ear before the second ring had a chance to complete its chimes. "Jeffries."

He instantly recognized the voice on the other end. It belonged to one of the members of the hastily formed task force, comprised of his men as well as several of the Bureau's special agents. So far, they seemed to be working rather well together.

"Hope you're having better luck over there than we are over here, Nick," Detective Robert Littleton said. "That interim sheriff they appointed, Tony Berretti, wasn't exactly all that pleased to have us ripping apart what's now his office."

"I already figured on that. Just remember, we're not in the business of pleasing small-time county sheriffs. We're after bigger things," Nick reminded Littleton.

Having come up against dead end after dead end, at this point Nick found himself dangerously short on patience. He felt as if his back was against the wall. He bit back a sigh as he dragged one hand through his dark, and at this point, unruly hair.

"Yeah, I know, which is why it would have been great if we had something to show for our efforts, but there's nothing here to give us so much as a clue that the guy was even *thinking* about blackmailing the 'honorable' senator from Dallas, much less doing it—or blackmailing anyone else."

Someone called to Littleton and he shouted back that he'd be right there before continuing with his "non-report" to Nick.

"And there's not a damn incriminating thing on his computer here. It's just lucky that you got hold of the one that Burris kept at his house," Littleton told him.

Nick could almost *hear* the relieved expression echo in the other man's voice.

"Yeah, lucky," Nick repeated. But they were going to need something more to corroborate "All right, Littleton, if you've got nothing to report, I'm hanging up. I'll see you later at the office."

He was about to terminate the connection when he heard Littleton call out to him.

"Um, Boss, if you don't mind, the guys and I are gonna call it a night and actually go home at six for a change." Littleton broached the idea slowly to his lead on the case. "My wife's been complaining a lot lately that I'm not spending enough time with her and the kids. She's got the kids calling me 'stranger' instead of Daddy."

Nick suppressed a laugh at this piece of information. He kept forgetting that although he had no family, the other men on his team did. He couldn't fault them for wanting to see them for more than a total of ten minutes a day.

"Fine, I'll call you if anything comes up," Nick said, then broke the connection as the man on the other end was thanking him.

He didn't need gratitude. What he needed was more evidence, something concrete. For all he knew, someone could have doctored Burris's home computer, planting damning evidence that would turn the dead man into a scapegoat. He needed something else to go on.

Preoccupied, he started to tuck the phone back into his pocket, but he wound up missing his target. The phone slipped from his fingers and fell onto the rug.

Hitting the floor at an angle, the phone bounced twice and wound up landing under Burris's desk.

All the way under.

"Great," Nick muttered, biting off a ripe curse in case either Suzy or her sister was passing by and could overhear him.

Getting down on all fours, Nick carefully crawled under the desk to retrieve his phone. The space was crammed and he had to be extra careful to keep from hitting his head.

The phone had landed at the extreme rear of the desk. Nick was forced to snake his way as far back as he was able to go.

He couldn't help thinking that as a kid, he would have really loved getting under a desk like this one, with only one side opened up the way it was. He would have spent hours playing under it, envisioning the desk to be a dozen different things, not the least of which would have been a cave.

The Bat Cave, Nick decided with an unconscious grin.

And, since he was away from any prying eyes, Nick allowed himself a momentary nostalgic respite as fragments of memories came back to him.

Memories of the little boy he'd once been before he'd become disillusioned with the world and found out that nothing ever turned out the way you expected or wanted it to.

But that time was years behind him, Nick reminded himself. Time to act like a responsible adult.

Phone in hand, he began to crawl backward out of the small spot. As he was snaking his way out, he thought he heard a landline ringing. Startled by the unexpected sound—half thinking it was coming from his own phone—he straightened abruptly and raised his head, only to smack it against the bottom of the drawer. Hard.

This time he did curse, although he managed to keep it under his breath, as pain shot through his skull and even vibrated along the bridge of his nose.

Moving carefully back one small "step" at a time, Nick glanced at the underside of the offending drawer to see if he had dented it—or left any blood behind.

And stopped short.

Unless he was hallucinating from the swiftly growing bump that was forming, there was something, a small padded envelope from what he could see, taped to the underside of the drawer.

Holding his breath, Nick began to work at peeling back the strips of tape and separating the envelope from the underside of the drawer.

The clear packing tape that held it in place was strong, which told him it was still relatively new. The weather in the area tended to be humid in the summer. The humidity was strong enough to leave its mark, corroding things like plastic shower curtains and plastic packing tape.

After finally freeing the envelope, Nick resumed backing out from the desk. He made sure not to lift his aching head until he was well clear of the desk. The top of his head was still throbbing from the sudden contact.

"Okay," he said to the envelope once he was clear and out in the open. "Let's hope you're worth this trouble and not just another so-called lead that's going to go nowhere."

Ripping the envelope open, he turned it upside down and shook it.

A single, thin, silver key fell at his feet. The

paper tag attached to it had a four digit number clearly typed on it.

The kind of number that was used to denote a bank safety deposit box.

Chapter 11

Nick studied the key thoughtfully for a moment, turning it over to see if the name of the bank had been embossed on either side.

He found nothing.

Still, he felt it safe to assume that it *was* a safety deposit key. He was just going to have to find out which bank housed the box.

Looking at it, he wondered if Suzy knew about the key. Its existence may have slipped her mind in the face of all this turmoil. Or she was deliberately holding back information. All things considered, he was rather a good judge of character, but he wasn't infallible.

Nick found the sheriff's widow in the kitchen, whipping up something that smelled incredibly tempting on three of the burners.

Almost as tempting as she was.

He *had* to get hold of himself. Otherwise, his thoughts would wear him down and there was no telling how he'd wind up acting on these feelings, which kept blindsiding him when he was least prepared.

Suzy looked up from the green peppers she was chopping into fine slivers. "What did you find?" she asked.

Habit made him feel her out warily. "What makes you think I found something?"

"You've got that look on your face, that look that says you came across another possible piece of the puzzle." She paused, waiting for him to disprove her assumption—or agree with it. When he didn't, she pressed, "Well, did you? Find something?" she specified, her eyes never leaving his face.

"Did your husband ever mention having a safety deposit box?"

Suzy thought for a moment. "He said something once about getting one," she recalled. "He said he thought we could keep life insurance policies and the deed to the house in it. But as far as I know, it was just talk." She saw what looked like a flash of interest flicker in Nick's eyes and second guessed what he was probably thinking: that maybe she'd had Peter killed to collect on the life insurance policy she'd just mentioned. "And, as far as I know," she said, reiterating a point she'd made when he'd first asked her about the life insurance policy, "there are no life insurance policies. That was just more talk on Peter's part."

Picking up the chopping block she'd been using, she tilted it and poured its finely chopped contents into the pot where she already had chicken breasts, parsley and mushrooms simmering in chicken broth.

"Maybe there were no life insurance policies, but it looks like there *is* a safety deposit box," he told her, holding up the key.

She stopped working and crossed to him. Wiping her hands on the apron she had carelessly tied around her waist, Suzy took the key from him and swiftly examined it, then handed it back to Nick.

"Never saw it before," she told him with a puzzled frown. "What do you think is in the box?"

Something that might have gotten Burris killed, but he kept that thought to himself for now, saying instead, "We're going to have to open it to find that out—and in order to open it, we're going to have to locate it."

"Well, I'm going out on a limb here, but seeing as how Vengeance isn't exactly a thriving metropolis, I don't think that's going to be overly difficult."

Her droll comment made him grin wryly. He wouldn't have thought she was capable of sarcasm. That she was amused him.

"Vengeance has two banks within the town limits. A lot of people are creatures of habit, so I'd start with the one where you have your checking accounts," he suggested. "Unless," he reconsidered for a second, "the sheriff was the type to try to hide his money in an offshore account somewhere, like in the Cayman Islands."

That *really* didn't sound like Peter, but then, this person who was emerging didn't sound like Peter, either, she thought, shaking her head.

"As far as I know," she told Nick, going back to the meal she was making on the stove, "he liked to keep things close by. I once told Peter I half expected him to keep our money under the mattress—for easy access. It wasn't that he really didn't trust banks," Suzy explained, "he just wanted to be able to get his hands on what he needed quickly, night or day."

Nick closed his hand over the key and tucked it into his pocket. "Nearby bank it is," he told her.

With a course laid out for them, Suzy was all set to take her apron off and drive to her bank, but one glance at the overhead floral kitchen clock on the opposite wall told her that going to the bank was not exactly an option right now.

It was seven o'clock, an hour after the bank had shut its doors. "It's closed," she realized with disappointment.

He nodded. "Nothing we can do until morning."

Suzy regrouped. "Well, we can eat dinner," she pointed out.

"There is that," Nick readily agreed, drawn closer to the stove by the aroma that was wafting over to him.

He recalled that he hadn't really been near a stove—other than in passing—since his divorce. He made coffee for himself in the morning, using a coffee machine he'd brought along with him on his move from Houston. If he wanted more, there was always a takeout restaurant in the area to call or drive to. The only items he purchased in the supermarket were coffee filters and coffee. The largest cans of coffee the market had to sell so that he could keep his trips there to a minimum.

He inhaled deeply—and appreciatively. "Smells good," he told her, nodding toward the pots on the stove.

Suzy smiled at the compliment. "I'm hoping it tastes better."

Hard as it was to believe, it did, Nick thought approximately forty-five minutes later. The meal Suzy had made tasted so incredibly good that he'd done something he rarely did. He overate.

He ate so much that if he consumed one forkful more, he wouldn't have been able to get up from the table and walk anywhere, much less to the front door.

He liked to think of himself as fighting trim. At this point though, he was more like pacifist fat. Or at least he felt that way, stuffed to the gills.

Suzy saw his empty plate and began to ask if he wanted another serving. "More—"

She didn't get a chance to finish her question because Nick held up his hand to halt the oncoming flow of words.

"No more," he told her. "Otherwise, I'm going

to burst at the seams right where I'm sitting. That was probably on* of the best meals I've ever had," he told her honestly.

His words surprised her and pleased her more than she could begin to say. "Thank you," she said when she found her voice. "You really didn't strike me as the type to hand out compliments like that."

Nick caught himself thinking that he liked the way that her eyes crinkled at the corners when she smiled broadly.

"I'm not," he told her. "I guess this just brought it out of me. It changed the rules," he added, trying to explain things to himself more than to her.

She was definitely a game changer for him. Being with her made him look at the world a little differently—made him feel more the way he assumed a normal person felt.

Made him think about and want things a normal man might want, instead of being the emotionless machine he had become in these last years.

You're waxing poetic, Jeffries. Time to go.

Taking a deep breath, Nick placed his hands against the table and pushed himself back. Abruptly, he said, "Bank opens at nine. I can be back here at a quarter to the hour if that's all right with you."

She nodded. "A quarter to nine is fine with me," she assured him. "I want to find out what Peter had in that safety deposit box as much as you do."

He'd only been looking at it from his own point of view, as a cop. What was this like for her, finding out over and over again that she was married to a virtual stranger? He was surprised that Suzy wasn't becoming increasingly bitter with every new discovery. He had felt bitter when Julie had been guilty of only one secret, not a score, like Burris seemed to be.

In her own way, Suzy Burris was made of sterner stuff than he was, Nick thought in admiration. He almost said as much to her, then caught himself at the last moment. He had to remember to keep this on a professional level.

"A quarter to nine tomorrow, then," he confirmed formally.

"I'll be ready," she promised.

But she wasn't.

When Nick arrived at her door the next morning, he found Suzy trembling, fighting to keep back tears. This was so different from the woman he'd left last night, he was instantly on the alert.

His hand went to his gun as he quickly scanned the immediate area, looking for an intruder.

"What's wrong?" he asked her sharply.

For a second, it was still all too fresh, too unnerving, and Suzy couldn't talk, couldn't organize what had just happened into coherent words.

Her heart was hammering hard in her chest, so hard that she thought it would literally break through her ribs.

Since there appeared to be no clear and present danger in the house, Nick removed his hand from his weapon and looked at the woman he had begun to think of as cool under fire.

This was definitely *not* cool under fire.

He saw the anguish in Suzy's eyes and he felt it twisting his heart. Before he could stop himself, Nick took her into his arms, his gruff voice transformed into a softer, infinitely more soothing one.

"Suzy, what's wrong?" he asked again, then coaxed, "Talk to me."

She willed herself to calm down as she took in a deep cleansing breath, and then let it out slowly. She had to do it a second time before she could even begin to answer him.

"I just had a phone call." She pressed her lips together to keep the sob that was hovering in her throat from coming out. "Someone just threatened Andy. He threatened my baby," she cried, her voice hitching. "He said that if I didn't hand over what Peter had on Senator Merris, what Peter had been holding on to as his 'insurance policy,' he was going to kill Andy."

Her voice shook now. "And he told me if I called the police, or told anyone at all about this, he was going to slit both our throats."

The senator again, Nick thought in exasperation. But the man was dead. Who the hell was calling if the senator was dead? Who was left to gain anything by getting their hands on whatever it was that Burris had stashed away? And what *was* it that Burris had had on the man? Compromising pictures? An incriminating tape?

Whatever it was, Nick had a hunch it was in that safety deposit box. The sooner they located it and opened it, the better.

Nick's arms tightened around her, as if to silently tell her that he was going to keep her safe, no matter what.

Because he was.

"No one's going to hurt you or your son," he told her fiercely. "I'm going to protect you. I swear I will." He needed her to try to remember everything she could about the call. "Suzy, this person who called you, did you recognize his voice? Did it sound familiar?"

Ashamed of her tears, she buried her face in his chest and moved her head from side to side in response to his question. A sense of hopelessness echoed in her voice.

"No, it was distorted." She raised her head to look up at him, her cheeks stained with tears as she struggled to regain control. "I can't even tell you for sure if it was a man or a woman. It was like being threatened by some mad, futuristic robot."

It sounded insane, but he knew what she was trying to say.

"For the time being, let's just assume it was a man. We need to find out what that key that your husband kept taped to the underside of his desk unlocks and what's inside. I have a feeling that it's going to be whatever this guy is looking for."

He knew what she was thinking, that the second they left for the bank, the person who called her would break into the house, harm her baby and her sister. "I'll have a patrolman keep an eye on things here while we're at the bank," he told her, taking out his phone.

Suzy let out a sigh and nodded her head. The

promise of a police officer on the premises didn't calm her down completely, but it was a start. If anything ever happened to Andy—or her sister—because of this, she wouldn't be able to live with herself.

Frank Kellerman smiled to himself. It was the kind of smile whose full impact sent chills through brave men's hearts and caused casual strangers to cross the street in order to avoid him and pretend he didn't exist.

The cold expression had served him well in his dealings as the late Senator Merris's head aide. Due to his dedication—and his less-than-upstanding dealings on his boss's behalf—he had clearly been on the rise. The senator saw him as an asset. Who knew how far he would have gone?

But then, according to new reports, someone had placed a plastic bag over the senator's face, suffocating him—and simultaneously sent all his well-orchestrated plans crumbling into the dust. He'd been filled with rage at the unfairness of it all, ready to lash out at the world and everyone in it.

And then, out of the blue, he'd been contacted by party or parties unknown. No names had been used, but the caller had known an unnerving amount of information about him. He'd been given specific instructions: retrieve the damning evidence that the late Sheriff Burris had had on the senator any way he could.

The disembodied voice on the other end of that fateful call had told him that if he served well, he'd go much further than he could possibly have ever dreamed.

Failure, the caller made it very clear, was not an option.

Kellerman wasn't planning on failing. Failure was for men without ambition or backbone. He had both—in spades—and he intended on going places.

He'd thought he'd get there after hitching his wagon to Merris's star, but obviously he'd been wrong there. The senator had gotten himself killed. For all his cunning, John Merris had ultimately turned into a loser.

Well, that wasn't going to be him, Kellerman thought fiercely.

As if to underscore that, out of the blue, he'd been given a second chance and he was going to make the most of it. Lightning had struck twice, it wasn't about to strike a third time.

Whoever had initially called and pressed him

into service was not going to be disappointed with his performance. He would get results. Hell, he'd had the sheriff's widow in tears, he could hear it in her voice. She wasn't about to risk her son's life and cross him.

Whatever it was that his mysterious caller was after, he'd be able to get it from the woman, despite her protests that she had no idea what he was talking about.

"Then *get* an idea," he had ordered in no uncertain terms, seeing through her innocent act. "Or your son dies. Your choice."

And with that, he'd hung up, confident that he had left her nerves in tatters. She'd be afraid not to comply with his order, it was as simple as that.

Satisfaction permeated all through him.

His feet were firmly back on the ladder of success and this time, he thought, shoving his hands into his pockets, he intended to climb up all the way.

About to leave the study where he'd gone to place the call, Kellerman stopped abruptly when his fingers came in contact with a folded piece of paper.

That hadn't been there the last time he'd worn

this jacket. As far as he could recall, the paper hadn't been there when he'd *put on* the jacket.

Puzzled, he pulled the paper out. It was folded over in a square and his first name was written across the top. Who the hell had put that into his pocket?

He looked around even though the room was empty. He half expected someone to pop out from behind the drapes, but no one did.

How did the note get into his pocket?

More curious than ever, he unfolded the paper. Printed inside were four words: "I'm proud of you."

An eerie feeling came over him. Someone was watching him.

But who? And where were they?

And exactly why were they proud of him?

He stared at the words for a very long time. The longer he stared, the less sense it all made.

Chapter 12

"Really, Andy and I will be fine," Lori assured her sister for a second time. "There's a patrolman on his way," she reminded Suzy, nodding at Nick for backup, since he'd been the one who'd placed the call. "You don't have to hold my hand until he gets here. Go, see what's in that mysterious safety deposit box," she urged. "You know I'm dying to find out myself."

But Suzy refused to budge. She stood by the window, looking out and waiting for some sign of an approaching police car. "The safety deposit box'll still be there if we leave fifteen minutes from now. I'm not going *anywhere* until I know you're safe."

"Can't you *make* her go?" Lori asked, appealing to Nick. "She's been overprotective and stubborn like this all her life."

"Well, if that's the case, nothing I say to her is going to change her mind and frankly, I'm afraid I agree with Suzy." Suzy flashed him a smile for his support. "That's why I called for a patrolman in the first place. It's better to be safe than sorry."

"He's here," Suzy announced, dropping the curtain back into place. "See," she said to Lori. "That wasn't so long, and now I don't have to worry about you."

"Ha," Lori jeered. "That'll be the day. You'd worry about me even if I had a ring of superheroes surrounding me."

"Shut up and take care of my son," Suzy said fondly, kissing her sister's cheek before she grabbed her jacket and purse.

The patrolman came in and, after a quick introduction to Lori, was briefed on his assignment. He was to park his vehicle in the driveway and make sure no one came anywhere *near* the house until they'd been officially cleared. The

FBI's temporary satellite office had been placed on speed dial.

"Feel better?" Nick asked her as they got into his car.

"Yes." Suzy was not oblivious to the fact that Nick hadn't pressured her either to give him back the safety deposit key, or leave the house before the patrolman arrived. She was grateful to him for that. "Thank you."

He made his way to the main road. "For what?" he asked her.

These past couple of days had taught her not to take *anything* for granted. "For not trying to get me to leave before your patrolman arrived."

Nick laughed shortly. "He's more your patrolman than mine." When he felt Suzy looking at him quizzically, he elaborated by making reference to the pledge each law enforcement officer took upon being sworn in. "Citizens are the ones the patrolman is supposed to 'serve and protect.' That's something we in the department take pretty seriously."

She thought of Peter and all the different ways she was discovering that he had failed to live up to that simple code.

"Too bad everyone doesn't," she murmured. For the sake of privacy, Nick pretended not to hear.

* * *

The bank manager at First National Bank of Vengeance appeared surprised when Suzy requested to see him. Other than when she had come in with her husband to sign the necessary papers when they had initially opened their checking and savings accounts, she hadn't been in. If there were any transactions to be handled, it was the sheriff who came in, not his wife.

Parker Stephens looked at her a little skeptically when she'd asked to be taken to the safety deposit box. "Would you happen to have your driver's license with you, Mrs. Burris? Protocol," he explained, flashing a shallow smile.

Suzy refrained from asking the bank manager why he'd think she wouldn't and instead just held it up for his examination.

He nodded, apparently satisfied, and flashed another forced smile. "Can't take people's word for things anymore, I'm sorry to say."

"No, you can't," Nick agreed crisply. "Can we hurry things along, please? Mrs. Burris would like to open her safety deposit box before Christmas."

The manager hesitated, seeming grossly uncomfortable about the situation.

"Something wrong, Mr. Stephens?" Nick asked him.

"Well, technically," the man hedged, "the safety deposit box belongs to the sheriff."

Nick's eyes narrowed. By now, everyone in town knew what had happened to the sheriff and the two other men. Did he expect the man to come back from the dead?

"Well, 'technically,'" Nick countered, his tone stern, his eyes steely as they pinned the bank manager in place, "the sheriff is dead. As his next of kin, not to mention his widow and cosigner on both accounts, Mrs. Burris is now entitled to have access to the safety deposit box in question."

For a moment, the bank manager appeared likely to contest Nick's statement, but then he seemed to visibly wilt and backed down. "Yes, of course. Come this way, please."

With that, Stephens led the way to the vault in the rear of the bank where the safety deposit boxes were housed. The sheriff's deposit box was Number 1094.

Although there was an entire wall devoted to safety deposit boxes, Suzy noticed that many of those doors were left wide open. Those were the boxes that were waiting for someone to put them to some use. Apparently most of First National's patrons had nothing they wanted to store or keep safe.

Turning to face her, the bank manager said, "I trust you have the key with you, Mrs. Burris."

She produced it and held it up before the man. "Right here."

With a nod, Stephens took hold of the key he wore on a long chain around his neck and inserted it into the larger of the two locks guarding the safety deposit box in question.

"Now you," he instructed. Once she inserted her key Stephens said, "Turn it, please."

He turned the bank's key at the same time and the lock gave. Dropping his key back to its place under his shirt, Stephens opened the door, slid the small box out and walked toward a booth off to one side that was actually three walls enclosed around a counter. He set the box on the counter and stepped back.

"Please call when you're done." And with that, Stephens retreated, leaving them alone in the vault.

The moment the bank manager was gone, Nick opened the safety deposit box. Inside he found a passport with the sheriff's picture, but not his name. It was issued to an alias. The passport was sitting on top of a white envelope.

Suzy took the passport from his hand and looked at it. It wasn't hard to put two and two together, even though she would have never thought it of him.

"I guess he was planning on a quick getaway without me," she murmured.

Suzy was surprised that the discovery bothered her, but it was more the idea of the deception rather than the thought of being abandoned by Peter that wounded her pride, she realized. No one liked the thought of being duped by someone.

It wasn't hard to guess what she was thinking. "The man was a fool in more ways than one," Nick told her flatly.

The comment had her looking at him sharply. Was that a compliment, or just a casual observation about the types of people Peter had most likely been dealing with? The fake passport indicated that he thought he had to be ready to pick up and run at a moment's notice.

Leaving her and the baby to fend for themselves. Since he had no other family, disappearing would have been easy.

Bastard, she thought.

Again she couldn't help wondering what was going on and just *who* Peter Burris—if that *was* his real name—actually was.

But she had no time to ponder the question any

longer because Nick had just opened the envelope and taken out its contents.

The envelope was filled with photographs. A great many photographs. Most of them were rather unfocused, some were even so blurred that it was hard to make out just what or who was supposed to be in them.

But others were definitely clear enough to make out.

And clear enough for the photographer and his or her subject to have them both convicted of treason against the United States.

Suzy's eyes narrowed as she looked at the top photograph. She recognized one of the men in it. "Is that—?"

He anticipated the name she was about to use and nodded. "Sure as hell looks like him," he confirmed. "He is one of the top known arms dealers in the world." To his way of thinking, it wasn't a ranking to be proud of.

The man he'd just mentioned had recently been implicated in a weapons trade with a country that didn't exactly make the U.S.'s top one hundred friends list. On the contrary, the country had been on the brink of war with the U.S. not once but several times.

Each time, the people in question had backed off because of a lack of sufficient firepower. But apparently the country was getting closer and closer to the point where that would no longer be a problem.

Suzy's eyes widened as she looked at another photograph. This time, there wasn't even a hesitation. "That's Senator Merris," she breathed.

"Not his best side," Nick commented dryly. "But this one's clearer," he said of another photograph he produced from in the stack.

She raised her eyes from the pile and looked at Nick. "Do you think Peter took these pictures?"

There were only two possibilities. "Either he did or he stole them from someone who did," Nick answered.

The photographs appeared to have been taken from a certain angle. Had the sheriff worn a spy cam on his person and let it roll automatically? Obviously, since the person who'd called Suzy had referred to them as "insurance," that was the way the sheriff had viewed them. They were something to use as leverage in case things went south.

Also just as obviously, Burris had never gotten a chance to use the photographs. Or maybe they were what had gotten him killed in the first place.

Suzy looked at Nick after they'd reviewed all the photographs. Many lives would be forever changed if these photographs saw the light of day. "What do we do with them?"

"I'm going to have to figure that out," he told her honestly. In their present situation, he wasn't sure just whom they could trust. He needed to do a little investigating before he came to any decisions. "For now, let's just leave them here. As long as you have the only key, they'll be safer here than in your house—or at the police station," he told her.

She nodded, feeling somewhat stunned at this latest discovery. Once again she couldn't help thinking how completely in the dark she'd been for most of her relationship with Peter. She would have never dreamed that he was involved in something like this.

What other secrets were waiting for her? she wondered uneasily.

Suzy fervently hoped that this was the last of the surprises. Right now it was just shock on top of shock and she wasn't sure just how much more she could actually take.

As they left the bank, Nick noticed how pale she appeared. All this was really rough on her. Sympathy stirred within him.

"Let's get you back home," he told her gently. "Give us both a chance to process this latest little development," he said wryly.

"Nothing to process," she told him, struggling not to sound exceedingly bitter. "I was married to a monster, a man who thought nothing of being a traitor to his own country." She raised her eyes to Nick's, daring him to contradict her. "Otherwise, he would have tried to stop what was going on in those photographs. At the very least, he would have sent them to a major newspaper or a national news channel, exposing the senator and those other people who're involved in those awful dealings." The moment the words were out, Suzy realized what her next course of action had to be. "That's what we have to do," she told Nick abruptly. "Get those photographs to the news media."

He understood where she was going with this and why. But things weren't that simple.

"Not yet," Nick cautioned. "This is just another piece of the huge puzzle and we have to see how it all comes together first. We can't afford to jump the gun," he warned, then promised her, "the pictures will definitely see the light of day. But not until we find out who killed your husband and the others."

She was convinced that it would be too late by then. With each breath she took, the feeling of impending doom continued to grow. And no matter what she did, Suzy just couldn't shake it.

The feeling grew even stronger when she and Nick arrived at her home. She noticed that the patrol car was still parked in front of her house.

But at first glance, the police officer who was supposed to be on duty appeared to be AWOL.

Nick pulled up his vehicle right beside the squad car and looked in. The patrolman wasn't AWOL, he was dead. One shot to the head at relatively close range. The killer was either cocky, or stupid. His money, Nick thought in frustrated anger, was on stupid.

Panic ripped through Suzy as she stifled the involuntary cry that rose to her lips. She was out of the car before Nick could stop her and she ran to the house.

The door wasn't locked.

"Suzy, wait!" Nick called after her angrily, his gun already drawn. "Damn it, listen to me," he shouted at her, fear getting the better of him.

He sprinted from the car to the house. Catching up to her, he grabbed Suzy by the arm and stopped her in her tracks before she could cross the threshold. There was no telling if the killer was inside, waiting for her.

"Getting yourself killed isn't going to help anyone," Nick snapped.

She didn't care about her own safety. It was her baby and her sister she was worried about.

"Lori!" Suzy shouted. "Lori, are you there? Answer me!"

The only answer was the echo of silence.

It was terrifying. This meant that her baby and her sister were gone—or worse.

"Stay here!" Nick ordered. His weapon poised, he moved into the house methodically, making sure each area was clear before going on to the next one.

"The hell I will," she retorted, shadowing his every movement.

He had no choice but to let her. There was no one to keep her back.

The scene that met them in the living room said it all.

A shattered lamp was on the floor, its pieces scattered, a side table was overturned and the playpen was glaringly empty.

Lori had obviously tried to fight off whoever had gained access to the house. Because the door hadn't been broken down or jimmied, the killer had probably posed as the police officer he'd killed. By the time Lori realized what was going on, it was too late. The killer was already in the house.

He'd kidnapped her sister and her baby.

"You said they'd be safe," Suzy cried, finally breaking down. "You promised, you promised," she sobbed, struggling not to crumble to her knees. The feeling of helplessness overwhelmed her.

Nick took her into his arms. She fought him, struggling to get free and then, suddenly utterly drained, she limply collapsed against him.

"We'll find them," Nick swore to her. "We'll find them."

She had no choice but to believe him. If she didn't, the hopelessness she felt vibrating within her would swallow her up whole, burying her.

What the hell is wrong with me? a voice inside her head demanded.

Since when did she fall to pieces like some fragile China doll? Lori and Andy *needed* her. There was no time for self-pity or sobbing. Crying and recriminations weren't going to save them. Getting her act together and looking for leads, for clues, so that she could come after them, *that* was going to save them.

Nick felt her suddenly straightening in his arms. He could almost *feel* Suzy rising to the occasion like some fictional super heroine rather than just falling to pieces.

What surprised him even more than this un-expected show of spirit and strength was his re-action to it. Not only did he admire this stronger side of Suzy, but he was turned on by the subtle display, as well.

It made him want her even more intensely than he had before.

"This is my family," she told him as she drew away and stood her ground. "It's up to me to find them." She lifted her chin defiantly. "This isn't your fight."

"The hell it's not," he countered. "We're in this thing together, and I intend to help find them and bring your sister and your baby back home whether you want my help or not."

There was a place for independence and for op-erating alone, but only a fool turned down knowl-edgeable help and she knew she could definitely use all the help she could get.

"Of course I want you," she responded with

feeling, then realized that a crucial word was missing and corrected herself. "I mean, of course I want your *help*." And then she tried to salvage the moment—and disarm it as well—by saying, "For one thing, your gun's bigger."

But it was too late. Both of them were aware of her slip of the tongue and what it meant: she'd told him she wanted him.

Just as he wanted her.

This, Nick realized, would be one tricky highwire act to negotiate.

"Let me call this in," he told her, taking out his cell phone, "and get some of the FBI's crime scene investigators out here. Maybe whoever did this obligingly left a print somewhere." He began pressing numbers on the keypad. He was going to have to call for an M.E., as well. Luckily—if that word could be applied to this case—the one sent in from Dallas was still here. "And then I'm getting you out of here."

She wanted nothing more than to get away, but she couldn't think about herself right now. There was just too much at stake. "What if they call? I don't want to miss it," she emphasized.

"They want what you have," he reminded her. It had to be the photographs in the safety deposit box. A lot of people were implicated in those photographs. A lot of careers would be ruined and a lot of people going to prison. "They'll call back. Right now, you need some time to pull yourself together. Some time to get in front of all this," he added.

So far, he judged, she was doing remarkably well, but that didn't mean she'd keep on going this way. Like someone who'd been shot and was still walking about, she hadn't felt the full impact yet and when she did, there was a possibility of complete collapse—far greater than what had almost transpired here.

Suzy fought back angry tears as she looked around the chaotic room. She should have been here to fight off the intruder. If she had been here, she could have kept Lori and the baby safe. For God's sake, she was stronger than Lori, she thought, upbraiding herself.

Get in front of all this. That was what Nick had just said.

If they didn't get Lori and Andy back, safe and unharmed, Suzy didn't think she would be able to get in front of all this.

Ever.

Chapter 13

As much as she wanted to go out and clear her head, feeling that any second now she would start climbing the walls, waiting for the kidnapper to call, she just couldn't make herself leave.

She stopped short of the threshold. When Nick looked at her, she shook her head and said, "I can't."

Knowing that to prod her might just push her over the edge emotionally, Nick nodded. "All right, I'll go get us some dinner," he told her.

She exhaled a breath. "Thank you."

"Nothing to thank me for," he answered. Calling in a patrolman to stay with Suzy, he left, promising to be back within the half hour.

The moment she saw Nick coming up the front walk, a little of her anxiety receded. It was as if only good things could happen as long as he was around. She knew it was a completely unrealistic attitude, but comforting nonetheless.

Nick came bearing several packages and was pleased that everything inside was still hot. He'd driven from the diner as if the very forces of hell were after him.

"Eat it while it's hot," he urged, depositing the various containers on the kitchen table and then opening them.

"You really didn't have to go to all this trouble," she protested. "I don't think I can keep anything down."

"But you'll give it a good try," he said in a voice that told her she really had no choice in the matter.

Suzy dutifully sat down once the plates and silverware were out. Nick had ordered two servings of baked ham, mashed potatoes and baby carrots drizzled with brown sugar and honey.

Taking first one bite, then another, Suzy was surprised to discover that not only *could* she eat, she was actually very hungry. One bite followed the other until suddenly there was nothing left on her plate.

Finished, she looked up at Nick with a touch of chagrin. He'd been right. Which meant he knew her better than she knew herself.

"I guess you called it."

Amused, Nick pretended not to know what she was talking about. "How's that again?"

He'd read her better than she'd read herself, Suzy thought. He deserved an apology, but she couldn't bring herself to muster one at the moment. Consequently, this was as close to one as he was going to get.

"When you said I was hungry." A rueful smile curved her mouth. "I guess I really was."

Nick had no need to hear an apology—he was just glad he could get her to finally eat something. "Just stands to reason that if you're going to keep pushing yourself so hard, you'll need to keep up your strength. Fastest way to do that that I know of is to remember to refuel. Eat," he told her, reducing the solution to one word.

And she had certainly done that, he thought. There wasn't so much as a crumb left on her plate. "Want anything else?" he asked. "Dessert? Coffee?" And then he shifted gears by asking, "Or would you like to have a drink?"

Suzy shook her head in response to each suggestion, although she hesitated for a moment when he mentioned the last item.

Part of her wanted to throw back a drink, or three, in order to numb the fear and pain that were so very close to the surface. She was so very afraid for her son's and sister's safety. But she knew that aside from it being only a temporary "fix" that actually fixed nothing, a drink, depending on its strength, could render her incapable of thinking clearly. And she needed to remain clearheaded just in case the kidnapper called back tonight— or Nick's team called with a lead for them.

"No, no drink," she finally said. "We'll have one together to celebrate once Lori and Andy are safe again."

"Sounds good," he responded, and she believed he meant it.

To her surprise, he helped her clear the plates and load them into the dishwasher. When they went back out into the living room, she couldn't help looking around, part of her expecting to see Lori there holding her son.

When she didn't, the pang that rose up within her was all but paralyzing. Tears rose in her eyes.

Nick saw the tears and knew what she was thinking. "We'll have them home before you know it." Promises like that were not typical for him, but he sensed she needed to hear the words.

"Home," Suzy echoed. The word sounded so empty to her. *Felt so empty*, she thought, looking around. "Right now it doesn't seem very much like home," she confessed freely. "Not after all that's happened."

Nick nodded. "I understand how you feel."

The words cut across her heart, drawing blood. She looked at Nick sharply as her temper suddenly flashed. Suzy couldn't keep the words back. "How could you possibly understand?" she asked, struggling not to lash out, not to shout at him for being so condescending as to assume he knew what she was suffering through. She wasn't being fair to him, but she didn't want this police detective patting her on the head as if she was a child, giving her platitudes. "My cheating, *dead* husband turns out to be a possible traitor, betraying not just me but his whole country as well and because of him, my sister and my son were kidnapped and who *knows* what else? Are you trying to tell me that happened to you, too?" she demanded hotly.

"No," Nick replied in a voice that was completely stripped of any emotion. He debated leaving it at that. He was, after all, a private person. But in the face of her pain, he decided to make the ultimate sacrifice and share his experience with her.

"I found out my wife was pregnant a week *after* she'd terminated her pregnancy. She'd swept that little life away without so much as passing thought, despite the fact that she knew I really wanted to have a family. When I called her on it, she told me that if I wanted to have something looking up at me adoringly, I should get a dog." He paused for a moment to purge the bitterness that always came along with the memory of that confrontation, then said, "I got a divorce instead."

Once the words were finally out, he realized that they—and the anger that propelled them—had been bottled up inside him all these long years, ever since he'd walked away from Julie that same afternoon he'd found out about what had happened to his unborn child. He'd never looked back. But the anger had lingered. And festered.

He felt almost liberated.

And just like that, her heart ached for him. "I'm sorry," Suzy whispered, emotion threatening to all but choke her windpipe.

It started to rain outside. The raindrops hitting against the living-room window made for a mournful sound, separating the two of them from the rest of the world.

"I didn't tell you that to get your sympathy—I told you to let you know that you're not the only person who's ever been blindsided by someone they thought they could trust. And if you ever repeat *any* of this," he warned her, "I'll deny it."

So he'd confided something to her that wasn't common knowledge. She found that comforting somehow, to be sharing a secret with him.

"I won't," she promised, then said in a slightly clearer voice, "And I'm still sorry. Sorry you didn't get a chance to find out what it feels like to hold your baby in your arms. But most of all, I'm sorry that I yelled at you just now. You're only trying to help me."

She dragged her hand through her hair, wishing she could organize her thoughts as easily. "I feel like my nerves have been peeled down to the very core, but that's still no excuse to take out my frustrations on you. You've been nothing but good and kind to me and I shouldn't be repaying you for that by going ballistic on you just like some kind of shrewish harpy—"

Nick held up his right hand for a second, calling a halt to Suzy's torrent of words. "Don't go painting wings and a halo on me just yet," he told her.

Suzy smiled at him, waiting for a second, just until the tears in her throat left so that she could talk. "Too late," she whispered.

But he heard her, even though he chose to say nothing, and just shook his head. On his *best* day no one would have *ever* accused him of being an angel.

"Well, I guess I'd better be going," he told her.

Her eyes widened. "You're leaving?"

"I'm not going very far," he answered. "If you need anything, I'll be right outside." He nodded in the general direction of his car. He intended on keeping vigil a few steps from her front door.

She shook her head, vetoing the idea. "The last policeman who stayed right outside my house didn't fare too well," she reminded him. "He wound up dead."

Her concern touched him even though he tried not to let it.

"I've pulled protective duty before," Nick assured her. "And I obviously lived to tell about it. Now, once I go out, I want you to lock up," he instructed. "I'll wait right outside the door until I hear you flip the locks and put the chain on."

She caught his hand as he turned to leave. He looked at her quizzically. Her eyes held his for a long moment. When she spoke, it was to make a request. "Come inside. Stay the night with me."

The way she said it, and the plea he saw in her eyes, left him no choice.

"Wait right here," he told her. Crossing to the door, he flipped first one lock, then the other, testing each individually before finally putting on the chain.

"I'll camp out on the couch," he began as he turned around to face her.

He supposed that he wasn't surprised by what came next. If he was honest with himself, on a subconscious level he'd seen it coming.

Because, on that same level, he'd been aware not just of Suzy's overwhelming vulnerability, but of his own, as well.

Something about the look in her eyes, the pain she was feeling not only *spoke* to him but also evoked memories of his own pain—the pain he'd thought buried along with all his unspoken hopes and plans for the future and for a family life.

Julie's heartless, thoughtless betrayal and the callous way she had erased all traces of their unborn child, not even pausing to think of the promise she was also erasing, had wounded his heart. To save himself and to stem the hemorrhaging flow, he'd literally denied his pain and sealed off that area of himself.

Sealed off all possibility of his feeling *anything* except a sense of duty and dedication to keep the citizens he served safe.

That was supposed to be enough.

It *had* been enough.

Until Suzy sealed her mouth to his.

Nick had no weapon at his disposal to try to hold her off. And rather than hold her off, he did the exact opposite. He eagerly sought the comfort, the warmth that she silently offered.

The flicker of momentarily unguarded pain she had seen in Nick's eyes reached out and touched her, communicated with her own pain and went so much further than merely letting her know that he'd endured hurt the same as she had.

It assured her that she wasn't alone. That he wasn't just there for her but he had *been* there—

where she was—as well. Reaching out to comfort him temporarily silenced her own pain.

Her own fears.

She desperately wanted something to blot out the overwhelming fear for her baby and her sister that made it hard for her to even breathe.

And then it was no longer about pain, about fear, about the waves of anxiety. It was stripped raw of all its layers and, at bottom, it was about the solace she discovered there, in Nick's arms, in his touch. In his kiss.

And she was ravenous for it.

Peter hadn't been a husband to her from the moment he'd learned that she had conceived. In withdrawing not just his attention and sexual contact, but any displays of affection as well, he'd made her feel like half a person, completely undesirable. She'd found herself adrift in loneliness.

More than anything, she now admitted, she'd craved a gentle touch, craved quiet, reassuring affection. Craved knowing that she mattered.

All these needs, wants, desires had seemed to burst to the surface the moment she and Nick walked into the house and closed the door. Unable to cope, to be alone with all these burdens she'd been carrying a second longer, Suzy threw her arms around the only lifeline she had.

Nick.

Every logical bone in his body told him this was wrong. That he couldn't go through with this. That he needed to separate himself from this woman he was so completely attracted to before he compromised not only her and himself, but his principles.

Nick knew he would regret this—for her sake— but he didn't care. He'd had regrets before. Better to regret a deed that was done than to regret never having done it at all.

He wanted to feel whole again, for however brief a time. Though it made no sense to him, for some reason, Suzy Burris made him feel whole. He'd sensed it almost from the moment he'd first laid eyes on her.

As was the case with everything in his life that didn't go by the book, he'd tried to bury it.

But it just wouldn't stay buried, not when she presented herself to him like this, all warm and willing, supple and wanting.

Nick was no match for that.

Nick was no match for her.

He kissed her over and over again, even as his brain ordered him to stop. He couldn't stop. It was beyond his control, beyond the spectrum of his power.

He needed what she had, what she gave, and a part of him tried to assuage his conscience by telling himself that she needed what he had to offer, as well. Comfort, affection and reaffirmation.

It wasn't a slow, languid dance the way he would have wanted it to be if it had been in his power to bestow on her. Instead, what was happening between them resembled a charged frenzy, underscored by articles of clothing now littering the floor, marking a path that went from the front door to the sofa several feet away.

And in the interim, as clothes continued to rain down, he kissed, caressed, touched and worshipped every square inch of her that he came in contact with, every single part of her body.

Firm and taut, her skin still felt like cream against his palms. He lost himself in that sensation. His heart raced as every kiss, every pass of his hand and hers bred a desire for more of the same.

No matter what he did, he couldn't seem to get enough of her. He found himself desperately wanting that final thrill yet just as desperately wanting this momentum they'd created to continue forever.

Or at the very least, awhile longer.

She didn't know what had come over her.

Maybe it was the abject loneliness. Maybe she just wanted to feel desirable again, to feel *something* other than pain, anger and weariness again. Peter had had her doubting herself, doubting her womanhood and even, these past few days, doubting her sanity and her ability to think clearly and make solid judgments. By his very actions—staying out late, hardly saying a word to her when he was home—he'd made her feel like a victim, unworthy of attention or affection or even the smallest kindness.

He'd begun to make her withdraw from life, which was when she'd decided she needed to save herself and divorce Peter.

But now, seeing herself in Nick's eyes, she saw a different image, a different person. Moreover, in Nick, she both saw and sensed a kindred spirit. He spoke to her soul, made her transcend the rubble she'd found all around her.

She'd never thrown herself at anyone before, never wanted anyone before the way she'd wanted Nick the moment they'd closed the door and sealed off the world.

Suddenly there had been nothing and no one, just him, just her. And the hurt that thrived within both of them grew smaller with each step she'd taken toward Nick, each kiss they'd shared so wildly.

It was almost an out-of-body experience for her. She was in awe of her own actions, of the liberties that she was taking. She'd always been faithful to the man she was with, and as Peter's wife, she'd been faithful to her vows. But Peter was dead and for the first time in a long time, she was not.

Nick brought out a wildness in her, and yet, there was this overpowering need for a connection. *He* was her connection.

To life, to love, to herself.

Every kiss seemed to flower into another one, creating equal partners of them even as she and Nick both tottered back and forth between being master and slave, captor and captive, each taking a turn at assuming all four roles.

When she felt she couldn't hold back anymore, couldn't wait a fraction of a second longer, Nick gathered her to him and, sealing his mouth to hers, he entered her, forming their union, making them one, a heartbeat before the rhythm of the act throbbed through both their bodies.

The tempo quickened with each passing second, each increasingly more zealous thrust.

Gasping and holding on to each other tightly, they leaped off the edge of the world and were suspended in space for an eternal moment. The euphoria surrounded them even as it pulled them back down to the earth.

And as they fell, she could feel his heart racing against hers.

She clung to that sensation, aware that all too soon, she would be at the mercy of her fears again, fears for her family's safety. But for this singular moment, she took comfort in the thought that she was with someone who cared about her as much as she cared about him.

Chapter 14

Slowly Nick's heart rate returned to normal, as did his ability to think.

And to own his actions.

Nick turned his head to look at the woman he was supposed to be protecting, not compromising. "You know, this *wasn't* what I had in mind when I agreed to spend the night in your house."

Her eyes met his. The euphoria had settled down to a comfortable glow within her. She knew she should be feeling guilty about this, but she couldn't. Peter had been dead only a few days, but he hadn't been her husband in close to a year.

There were no ties there, no promises that she'd broken by making love with Nick.

She smiled at him now. "I know."

As far as Suzy was concerned, she knew that she had made the first move. It truly *was* a first move on her part because she'd never done anything like that before, never literally thrown herself at a man before. But there had been something, a bond, a kindred spirit she'd sensed between the detective and herself that had removed the barriers.

But while there was no guilt for making love with Nick so soon after Peter's death, something else hit her hard, broadsiding her when she least expected it.

He saw the tears in her eyes. "What's wrong?" he asked, concerned. "Did I hurt you?"

She shook her head, afraid to speak, afraid that she would sob if she did.

"Tell me," he coaxed softly.

It took her a moment more to gain control over herself. "What kind of monster *am* I?" she cried. "My son and my sister were kidnapped. Right now they're at the mercy of some deranged lunatic—or worse," she sobbed angrily. "And what am I doing? I'm throwing myself at the police detective who's investigating my husband's murder."

Nick drew her into his arms, holding her as she struggled against him. Suzy finally just crumbled, her tears flowing freely.

"You're not a monster," he told her. "You're a human being. And human beings need comforting when they're in the middle of a stressful situation, the way you are. Suzy, you did nothing wrong," he assured her, his voice low, reasonable. Comforting. He wiped away her tears with his thumb. "It's going to be all right, Suzy. I promise. We'll find them and get them back."

She knew he couldn't really guarantee that, but just as before, she clung to his words, to the idea that somehow, some way, they were going to find Lori and her baby.

She'd made love with him in order to stop thinking, but there was more to it than that. She'd made love with Nick because he made her feel that she wasn't alone.

And she was grateful to him for that. But she didn't want him to think she was some sort of a clinging vine.

Taking a breath to steady her nerves, she told him quietly, "This isn't going to develop into a pattern."

The remark seemed to come out of the blue,

catching Nick off guard. Was she warning him off, or saying that for his benefit? How did he tell her that he wouldn't mind if it did become a pattern? That making love with her had opened doors and windows inside him and had allowed the sun to come in for the first time in years?

He didn't want Suzy to feel he was crowding her, as if he expected anything more from her, even though he would have welcomed it.

He didn't want to scare her.

Going on instinct, he just continued holding her.

"You talk too much," he told her quietly.

Maybe she did, Suzy thought. "Makes up for you hardly talking at all."

Amused, Nick laughed quietly and brushed what was intended to be nothing more than a fleeting, chaste kiss against her lips. But he discovered the second that contact was reestablished, when it came to this woman, there was no such thing as fleeting, no such thing as chaste. He'd opened up the floodgates again and gotten himself swept away.

He had no choice but to swim for his life.

He did it with pleasure.

She woke up alone.

The moment Suzy opened her eyes, the languid feeling had vanished.

Startled by the silence that all but smothered her, she bolted upright.

She was still in bed.

Her bed.

Last night came back to her in fits and starts, accompanied by a wave of heat. They'd made their way to her bedroom where they must have fallen asleep after making love again. Twice.

But where was Nick?

She listened intently—and heard nothing but more silence.

Tumbling out of bed, Suzy grabbed the robe that must have fallen to the floor sometime during last night's very passionate activities. As she shrugged into the robe, slipping it over her nude body, she saw the folded paper on the bureau.

Knotting the sash at her waist, she crossed to the bureau and quickly skimmed the note.

"Went to follow up a lead. There are two detectives posted in a utility van across the street. They'll keep you safe. I'll call you soon. Nick."

How could he have left without her?

"What lead?" she asked the note, exceedingly frustrated as she slipped the paper into her robe's pocket. "And when's 'soon'?"

He hadn't marked down a time on the note,

hadn't indicated when he'd written it, so she had no way of gauging just what he meant by "soon."

Why hadn't he woken her up? She would have gone with him instead of staying behind, to spend the next excruciatingly endless hours perched on the sharp ends of pins and needles, waiting to hear something, *anything*.

From him.

From the kidnapper.

Waiting to learn if her baby and her sister were safe, or if something had happened to them because she had made an unforgivably horrible mistake and gotten involved with the wrong man.

And, by everything she'd come to discover, Peter Burris was definitely the wrong man.

Forcing herself to go through the motions of living, of actually being able to function, Suzy took the fastest shower of her life. As a precaution, she'd brought both her cell phone and a portable phone connected to her landline into the bathroom so she'd be able to hear either one if they rang.

They didn't.

Feeling increasingly more helpless and frustrated, Suzy got dressed and went downstairs. Her intent was to get some coffee and hope that it would somehow jump-start her energy and push the anxiety she was experiencing into the background.

When she came to the bottom of the stairs, she saw what looked like another note in the foyer on the floor. It had obviously been slipped under the front door.

Had Nick written her a second note before leaving?

The moment she picked up the note and looked at it, she knew this wasn't from Nick. Moreover, it had to have been slipped under her door after he'd already left, otherwise, she was certain that at the very least, he would have put it with the other note.

There were only four words on this one written in a flowing, flowery script:

He loved me more.

The person—most likely a woman—who had written this note had to be talking about Peter.

Suzy clenched her hand into a fist. Angry, feeling as if she was about to lose her mind, Suzy started to crumple up the note, then stopped herself. Nick would want to see this and have it analyzed for possible prints. Any satisfaction she might have gotten from tearing the note into tiny bits would have to be put on hold. Evidence took precedence over everything else.

"Damn you, Peter. And damn me for not seeing any of this," she cried, suddenly feeling very close to tears.

He's not worth it.

No, he wasn't. But Andy and Lori were.

Suzy let out a shaky breath. Without knowing where Nick had gone, she had no choice. She was forced to remain exactly where she was and hope that the kidnapper would get in contact with her. She needed him to call with instructions, telling her what she had to do in order to get Andy and Lori back.

Suzy went into the kitchen to make coffee. She definitely needed the distraction—and the caffeine.

She was surprised to discover that the coffee was already made. Nick had obviously left it brewing for her. She found this fact immensely comforting even though she wouldn't have been able to explain to anyone exactly why.

"Think he killed them?" Juarez asked Nick.

It was his first day back. He'd brought cigars with him to hand out to everyone, following an age-old tradition passed on to him by his fore-bearers. In addition, Juarez had brought a stack of photographs of his newborn son with him and was proudly showing them to anyone and everyone who came within fifteen feet of his desk.

He'd arrived just as Frank Kellerman, the late senator's chief aide, was brought in and placed in the interrogation room.

Nick had done the interview, and then had come out, leaving Kellerman sitting in the room by himself.

For the time being, Nick just wanted to study the man through the one-way glass, wanted Kellerman to wait and wonder if there was more coming.

In a lot of the cases he'd dealt with in Houston, the suspects did a far more effective job on themselves, anticipating the worse and working themselves up.

"I don't think he actually killed any of them," Nick answered. "But I'd bet a month's pay that he's guilty of *something*. Innocent men just don't fidget like that. He could hardly sit still throughout the whole interview."

As he and Juarez looked on, the aide on the other side of the glass was all but tap-dancing at the table. His feet and legs seemed to be moving almost independently of his upper torso. The rest of him shifted nervously in his seat, first over to one side, then to the other—and back again.

Juarez readily agreed, pointing out, "Look at the way he's fidgeting."

"That's way more than fidgeting," Nick agreed. "If he were a rocket, he'd be set to launch any second now."

Too bad there was no concrete evidence right now enabling them to hold the aide. They would have to let him go soon, he thought grimly, searching for a way he could use that to his advantage.

"Guilty conscience?" Juarez guessed.

"He sure as hell is guilty of something," Nick responded. The trouble was, guilty of what? "And scared."

"Of us?" Juarez smirked.

Nick shook his head. "Not us. He's afraid of whoever he's working for," was his guess. Glancing at his watch, Nick knew they'd run out of time and they had nothing on the man to hold him any longer. "I'm going to go get a coffee out of the vending machine. You let Kellerman go."

That wasn't what the younger detective had expected to hear. "Just like that?" Juarez asked, stunned.

"No, not just like that," Nick amended. "I plan to tail the S.O.B. and see if he winds up incriminating himself somehow." He glanced back into the interrogation room. "He knows more than he's telling, and I intend to find out just what, even if I have to follow him to hell and back," he told Juarez as he walked away to the vending machine.

Suzy nearly jumped out of her skin when her landline finally rang.

Her heart hammering wildly, she picked up the receiver with both hands to keep from dropping it, then placed it to her ear. "Hello?"

"One ring." The sound of harsh laughter met her ear. "You must be anxious."

It was him.

The kidnapper.

The man with the metallic-sounding voice.

Suzy ordered herself to hold it together. She knew she needed to sound as if she were calm and in control, if not of the situation, of at least herself. Otherwise the man on the other end of the call would know he was holding all the cards and that could prove fatal for Andy and Lori.

But her voice almost broke as she demanded,

"Let my sister and my baby go. They're not part of it."

"Oh, but they are, Mrs. Burris, they are. They're my leverage. Otherwise, you won't do as I say and you'll think that boyfriend of yours can keep you safe. By the way, did you have a nice night together?" he asked her knowingly. "I see it's true what they say about still waters." The laughter unnerved her, getting under her skin. "My, my, but you really are a wildcat."

Her heart all but stopped as embarrassment flooded her cheeks. This monster who was talking as if he'd witnessed everything that had happened here last night. But how could he?

"How did you—"

"I have eyes everywhere, Mrs. Burris, which is why I'll know if you try to get in contact with your detective boyfriend after we hang up." His voice turned malevolent as he went on to warn her, "Things will go very badly for your little family if you do. You won't want them to wind up like your husband now, do you?"

Fear ripped right through her heart. "No, no, I don't. I'll do anything you want," she cried, "just please, please don't hurt them."

"All right, I'm not a monster, Mrs. Burris. I

can be reasoned with." The man on the other end paused, shifting gears. " Now listen very carefully. I want you to slip out of the house without alerting those detectives in the van. Once you're clear of them, I want you to go get that envelope you found in the bank's safety deposit box—don't stop to make any copies. I'll know if you do," he said ominously.

"I won't make any copies," she promised. "Just tell me where you want me to bring the envelope."

But rather than tell her, he laughed again, no doubt enjoying himself and this torturous game he was playing.

"One step at a time, Mrs. Burris. One step at a time. And remember," he underscored darkly, "if you tell your boyfriend—or anyone else about this—they die. You make copies of a single photograph—they die. You don't follow all my instructions to the letter, they—well, I think you get the picture by now." He laughed at his own little joke. "Get it? The picture."

She let out a long, shaky breath, loathing the person on the other end with every fiber of her being. But for Lori's and Andy's sakes, she was forced to play along, to feign admiration.

"I get it," she said between clenched teeth. "Very clever."

"Yes, I am," he agreed. "Glad you realize that." And then he seemed to shift gears, for the moment tiring of the cat-and-mouse routine. "All right. You have an hour before the bank opens. Have yourself a nice breakfast, *then go get the envelope,*" he ordered gruffly. "And wait for my call."

The line went dead.

Have yourself a nice breakfast.

As if she could keep anything down, Suzy thought angrily. Her stomach was so knotted up, she was amazed she could still breathe.

Suzy looked at her watch. It was only ten to eight. Early. But she might as well drive over to the bank and wait in the parking lot for it to open its doors. This way, if Nick came back before nine, she wouldn't have to come up with any excuses about where she was going or why she didn't want him with her.

If he knew the truth, there was no way he'd let her go alone—besides, she had no doubts that the kidnapper *was* watching her every move. There had to be cameras planted in her house.

In her house she thought angrily, feeling horribly violated. Who had done that? And when?

Could Peter have put the cameras up? Why? Was it to keep them safe, or to spy on her? She'd never given him any reason for the latter, but she was beginning to think there didn't have to be a reason for some people to do criminal things.

Her head *really* began to ache. It felt as if her skull were being cracked in two.

Running on adrenaline, she decided to make her escape from the house via the side yard. There was a gate that opened behind some garbage pails. The detectives in the van were watching for someone breaking in, not sneaking out. It was her only hope, and with a little bit of luck she could get away. From there, she could call a cab to take her to the bank.

Just as she was about to leave, the phone rang again.

It took effort to stifle the involuntary scream. Bracing herself, Suzy picked up the receiver. Was it him again? Had he changed his mind about making her pick up the envelope for some reason? It was too soon for the call naming the drop-off point. He knew she hadn't gone to the bank yet.

Suzy could feel herself trembling inside as she said, "Hello?"

"Hi."

Her shoulders tensed for another reason entirely when she realized it was Nick calling and not the kidnapper. Her mind scurried about, trying to come up with something she could say to make the kidnapper think she was warding Nick off while still leaving him a clue.

Nothing was coming to her.

"I know I left rather abruptly," Nick said, "but one of the men on the joint task force found some evidence that might have implicated one of the late senator's aides and we brought them all in for questioning." He paused as if to let all this sink in. "I'm not sure when I can be there, but the minute I wrap this up, I'll be over and—"

"Don't bother," she snapped. "I don't need you coming over." Her voice rose with each word she uttered. "I don't need you hounding me every minute. Why don't you do something productive, like find my husband's killer and put him in jail?"

This sounded nothing like the woman he'd been with last night. Had the kidnapper called her? If he had, wouldn't she have told him that immediately? Why was she responding like that?

"Suzy, is something wrong?"

"Wrong?" she jeered. "What could possibly be wrong? Everything's just ginger-peachy—as long as you leave me alone," she added, adding a nasty edge to her tone. "Go do your job, and I'll do mine, understand? Go do your job!" she shouted and with that, she banged down the receiver, terminating the call and praying that Nick would realize what she was really trying to tell him instead of just think that she had gone off the deep end. That, she hoped, was the way she meant for the kidnapper to interpret what had just gone down.

Hopefully, Nick was smarter than the kidnapper.

"Wow, I could hear her yelling all the way over here," Juarez commented, looking at his partner as he came forward. "You really must have done something to tick her off."

Nick didn't answer Juarez. He felt like a man who had just been handed the ultimate puzzle. He stared at the phone thoughtfully, trying to make sense out of what had just happened. He had an uneasy feeling that if he was slow in figuring it out, it would be too late.

His cell beeped. Flipping it open, he saw the text. The man he had following Kellerman just alerted him that the senator's right-hand man was on the move.

Nick frowned. He knew what he had to do. For the time being, no matter how much he wanted to go see her and find out what was going on, Suzy's puzzle would have to wait.

Nick had gotten into his car and had just turned the ignition when his cell phone beeped again.

Now what? he wondered impatiently.

Pausing, he took his phone out again and looked at the text message. One of the detectives he'd instructed to keep an eye out on Suzy had sent his own message. Suzy had just been seen sneaking out of the side yard and getting into a cab down the block.

Chapter 15

Janice Maxwell was considered by one and all to be the perfect administrative assistant. She came in early, left late and in between handled both daily routines and emergencies with the same aplomb and maximum efficiency. No one at Darby College could remember ever seeing the stately, fortysomething woman acting as if she was even the least bit ruffled or upset.

She was the eye of the storm, the one everyone, including her employer, Dean Abramowitz, turned to when they needed the opinion of someone who was calm and levelheaded.

Which was why, when Janice Maxwell suddenly burst into the dean's office, looking white as a sheet and clearly seven degrees beyond upset, the dean fully expected that, at the very least, the devil himself was on her heels.

But she was alone, as well as breathless and apparently speechless.

"Ms. Maxwell, what is it? What happened?" he demanded. Never in their long history together had the woman *ever* burst into his office without first knocking, and then waiting for permission to enter.

His nerves were already fairly shot, what with Melinda Grayson's undeclared kidnapping and then those grad students finding the three murder victims just outside of the school grounds.

Dean Abramowitz was afraid even to hazard a guess as to what had brought on Ms. Maxwell's highly unusual break with decorum.

"Answer me!" he instructed. "What the devil is going on here?"

Rather than say a word, the tall, thin woman who appeared to be all angles, quickly came around to the dean's side of the computer and proceeded to elbow him out of the way despite his protests. The moment she did, she took control of his keyboard, her fingers flying over the keys.

"What the hell's gotten into you, woman?" Abramowitz indignantly shouted. He was strongly debating calling Campus Security and having her taken away.

"Look!" She choked out the single word, turning the monitor so that he could get a better view of the video she'd just pulled up. A video that, according to the number of hits indicated in the corner, had gone insanely viral.

The dean didn't have to ask her, "At what?" The video Janice Maxwell had just pulled up commanded his complete, undivided and utterly horrified attention.

Abramowitz stared, openmouthed, as a terrified Melinda Grayson, her hands and feet tied securely to a chair, pleaded with someone just off camera not to kill her. She was sobbing almost uncontrollably.

The dean's body was as tense as a fireplace poker as he watched someone's hand suddenly dart out to strike the professor across the face.

Just as contact was about to be made, the screen went black.

The whole video lasted a total of thirty seconds.

It felt as if time had stopped while he watched.

His eyes huge, Abramowitz looked at his administrative assistant. The woman who ordinarily brought order to chaos had succeeded in doing just the opposite to his life.

"Where's the rest of it?" he asked, waiting for the video to start up where it had left off.

Ms. Maxwell shook her head. Her voice, when she spoke, was hardly above a choked whisper. "That's all there is, Dean."

His hands shaking, Abramowitz took a card out of his jacket pocket and began to dial Detective Nick Jeffries's number.

Nick looked at the caller's name on his cellphone screen as it rang.

It was Dean Abramowitz.

Again.

Undoubtedly calling to find out if he'd discovered anything new. The dean had been calling him on the average of four, five times a day since he'd questioned him about both the professor's disappearance and the three murder victims. As per his habit, he'd left his card with the educator, asking him to call if he happened to remember something else about either case. Instead, the dean would call to quiz *him,* wanting to know if any progress had been made in the investigation into the professor's disappearance.

After the first few calls, Nick had told Abramo-witz that he would be able to spend his time more wisely *investigating* the case rather than updating him on it. For a dean, the man was rather thick. He hadn't taken the hint.

Right now, Nick didn't have time to hold the dean's hand or reassure him that they'd find the professor as well as whoever had killed those three men. In his book, actions spoke louder than words.

He let the call go to voice mail.

Please let them be all right, please let them be all right.

The single sentence kept repeating itself in Su-zy's head over and over like an endless loop as she drove, first to the bank to retrieve the envelope in the safety deposit box, then to the address she'd been given. The metallic voice on the phone had called with the drop location approximately five minutes after she had gotten the envelope with its photographs out of the safety deposit box.

Was he watching her somehow? Had he planted a camera in her car? Suzy wondered uneasily, looking around the interior of her vehicle. The thought that this man was spying on her sent chills down her spine and all but cut off her air supply.

She forced herself to get her mind back on the only thing that mattered: saving Andy and Lori. She'd find a way to deal with the man who was torturing her this way later.

The address she'd been given turned out to belong to an abandoned storefront in the more rundown section of town. It had once served as a satellite campaign office when Senator Merris was aggressively running for reelection. An old campaign poster, faded from the sun and hanging at half-mast, the tape in the upper corners no longer able to support it, was still in the window, forgotten by whoever had been charged with cleaning up that particular go-round.

Getting out of the car, Suzy approached the empty looking storefront and tried the door. She expected it to be locked, but it easily gave beneath her hand.

Suzy took a deep breath to at least *partially* steady her nerves. She pulled the door open, braced herself and then walked in.

The smell of dust and mold assaulted her nose the second she walked in. She let the door close behind her as she looked around.

"Hello? Is anyone here?" Suzy called out.

Only the echo of her own voice as it bounced off the emptiness answered her.

Had she gotten the address wrong? Was the kidnapper jerking her around, sending her to the wrong place to show her that he was holding all the cards and that she had none?

But she *did* hold a card, Suzy silently insisted. She had the photographs. The ones he apparently was so desperate to get his hands on. That had to be worth something.

She dug in, holding her ground and giving it one more try.

"Look, I came here just like you told me to. I have the photographs. Now stop playing games and show yourself, damn it!" she demanded.

There was still no answer, but she couldn't shake the feeling that she was being watched. What was this creep's game?

"Okay, have it your way," she declared, retracing her steps to the door. "I'm taking these photographs straight to the newspaper office. I'm sure they can find a place for some of them somewhere on their front page."

She willed herself to turn around and start to go out the front door.

"Stay where you are!"

But rather than freeze, the way the man clearly wanted her to, Suzy swung around to face whoever had called out the order.

She didn't recognize the man standing there.

He was the kind of man, Suzy realized, who easily faded into the woodwork and could, just as easily, fade from memory five minutes after he left a room. It didn't seem possible that someone so nondescript could have taken her sister and her child, but then, she was discovering as more things about Peter's dual life came to the surface, that *anything* was possible.

Especially that which seemed to be impossible.

With quick, angry steps, the man crossed to her. "Give me the photographs!" he demanded.

She'd stuffed the whole thing into her oversize shoulder bag just before she'd left the bank and now angled her purse so that it hung behind her, out of his initial reach.

"First let me see my sister and my baby," she countered.

"You're in no position to dictate terms," he growled malevolently at her.

Rather than shrink away, Suzy raised her chin defiantly and retorted, "We've got a difference of opinion here, because I think I am. Now, you're not getting your hands on *anything* until I see my son and my sister with my own eyes."

Agitated—this was *not* going according to plan—Frank Kellerman cursed at her, and then grudgingly said, "All right, they're in the back room."

Tying Lori up like a Thanksgiving turkey, he'd left her and the baby in what had once been the senator's office whenever the man had swung by his smaller campaign headquarters.

Kellerman meant for her to follow him, but Suzy remained exactly where she was. She was not about to allow this man to get behind her for any reason. If she did, she thought, she'd deserve just what she got. The man had *psychotic* written all over him.

"Bring them out," Suzy told him. "I'll be right here. Waiting."

Kellerman's eyes narrowed, all but shooting lightning bolts. "Don't dictate terms to me," he shouted.

"Take it as a request, then," she retorted. There wasn't even so much as a hint of friendliness in her voice. She placed her cards on the table. "When I see with my own eyes that they're all right, *then* I'll let you have the photographs," she promised.

He said nothing for a moment, his eyes raking up and down her body. "You've got guts," he told her with what amounted to the thinnest trace of admiration.

She supposed that in his world, he was flattering her. Maybe even flirting with her. But in her world, he was a stomach-turning lowlife who couldn't be trusted and she wasn't about to let her guard down.

The man was a psychopath, she thought.

"I've got the photographs," she pointed out, knowing that to him, that was all that mattered.

"Stay here," he ordered.

She'd gotten her way. But there was no time to savor the victory. It was on to the next battle, the next confrontation. But for now, she promised, "I won't move a muscle."

"Yeah, you will," he smirked as he whirled around, a gun in his hand. He raised it quickly, his intention clear. He would kill her and take the photographs.

And then, just like that, he was aiming his gun at her. There was no place to run, no place to hide. This crazy person was going to kill her.

The thought that she had less than a minute to live galloped through her head.

But just as she braced to be killed, she heard the kidnapper scream. It was a pain-riddled cry, not a triumphant battle charge.

The man who would be her killer crumpled to the floor right in front of her, the blood flowing from his shoulder hitting the floor at the same time that he did. When his knees made contact with the floor, they immediately began to absorb the blood, discoloring his very expensive suit.

Stunned, not knowing what to think, Suzy turned around to see where the life-saving shot had originated. It seemed to be from directly behind her, but there was no one there, only the empty storefront window and the curling poster.

That was when she saw him.

Nick, sprinting toward her, a rifle held tightly in his hand. Throwing the door open so hard it banged on the opposite wall, he demanded, "Are you all right?" in a tough, no-nonsense voice.

"I'll let you know when I stop shaking inside," she answered. A hundred different questions popped up in her mind, all simultaneously piling on top of one another. "Did you just shoot him?" she asked, amazed at the accuracy of the shot he'd taken.

When Nick nodded in response, she still couldn't make sense of it. That seemed like an impossible shot.

"But how?" she demanded. "There was no one out there when I walked in." She scrutinized him, completely stunned by what he'd just managed to do. "Just what kind of superpowers do you have, anyway?" As far as she was concerned, it would have taken someone with exceptional vision to nail that shot. Why hadn't he mentioned being a sharp-shooter to her?

Because the man doesn't like to call attention to himself, that's why. Don't you know anything about the man? Apparently not, but she was will-ing to learn.

The aide was conscious and groaning pitifully, in between emitting squeals, complaining of al-most being killed. He let loose a string of profan-ity, declaring that he was at death's door.

"You killed me," he sobbed angrily. "I'm thirty years old and you killed me!"

Jerking the man up to his feet none too gently, Nick answered Suzy's question simply, "I was a sniper in the marines."

She had more questions for him, a lot more, such as how he knew she was there, but they could all wait until she got the answer to one question out of the man Nick had taken prisoner.

"Where are they?" she demanded angrily. "Where're my baby and my sister?"

Kellerman countered by demanding, "Get me to a hospital. I'm bleeding to death here."

Nick grabbed Kellerman by his shoulder, sending a fresh wave of pain shooting right through the man down to his very core.

"Haven't you heard?" Nick asked sarcastically. "Only the good die young. Which means you're not going anywhere but to jail."

"I need a doctor!" Kellerman sobbed, his knees buckling.

Nick was unmoved, his eyes ominous as he regarded the babbling aide. "Tell us where her sister and baby are, and I'll see what I can do about that hospital."

It was obvious that under different circumstances, Kellerman would have loved nothing better than to keep that piece of information from either of them, but he was growing weaker and he could see the blood oozing from his wound. He was afraid that the detective would just leave him handcuffed here to die.

"All right, all right, I already told you where they are," he grumbled, jerking one thumb toward the rear of the building. "They're in the back room."

Suzy didn't even wait for Nick.

She flew to the back office of the defunct campaign center. Scanning the area, she saw a single closed door and made for it. The door was locked. Infuriated, frightened, she didn't even wait for Nick. Instead, she managed to kick it hard enough to get the door off its hinges.

Tears sprang to her eyes as she found herself looking at her only family. Lori was bound and gagged and tied to a chair. Andy was on the floor, his eyes shut.

Terror instantly shot through her as Suzy dropped to her knees and gathered her son to her. The next moment, the terror abated when she saw the infant stir and open his eyes.

"Oh, Andy, you're alive. You're alive," she cried as tears of relief and joy filled her eyes, and then spilled out.

With Andy nestled against her, she turned toward her sister to free her. But by then Nick had come in and he quickly made short work of the ropes holding Lori bound to the chair and the duct tape over her mouth.

The second the gag was off her mouth, Lori cried, "Where's that horrible man?"

Apprehension vibrating in every fiber of her being, Lori was looking past Nick, searching for Kellerman. At this point, she was afraid that he would burst into the room and kill them all, just as he'd threatened her he'd do, once her sister came for them.

"On his way to the jail soon. The man I asked to tail Kellerman called for backup. They just got here. Don't worry. Kellerman's not going to be a threat to any of you anymore," Nick assured her as he removed the last of the rope from her wrist, doing it as gently as he could. He still heard her suck in her breath, stifling a cry. "Sorry about that," he apologized.

"You just freed my nephew and me, trust me, you have nothing to be sorry about, Detective," Lori told him as she rubbed her wrists and tried to get the blood flowing through them again.

"How did you know I would be here?" Suzy asked Nick as she continued to hug Andy to her.

The way she felt right at this moment, she didn't think she would ever be able to let her son go.

"I didn't know," he told her. "I followed you here. After that tongue-lashing you gave me," he explained, "I knew something had to be up." Since Lori was within earshot, he refrained from adding that he thought her behavior particularly suspect after the night they'd just shared.

Suzy blew out a breath, happy that Nick had managed to catch on quickly instead of thinking she was just some nut job with a screw loose.

"I don't know how I'll ever be able to thank you," she told him sincerely.

He grinned at her, more relieved that she was unharmed than he could ever begin to put into words. "Oh, I'll think of something," he promised her.

A warm feeling began to mingle with the one of utter relief. Her eyes crinkled as she smiled at her lover and the protector of her family.

"If you don't, I will," she promised.

Chapter 16

Suzy moved to one side, getting out of the way as the EMTs Nick summoned wheeled the unconscious Kellerman out of the abandoned campaign headquarters. The ambulance, its lights momentarily dormant, was waiting just outside the front door.

As a precautionary measure, one of the paramedics had also checked out Lori and Andy, pronouncing them to be none the worse for their harrowing ordeal. Andy had even fallen asleep right after the paramedic had finished.

Lori had taken the sleeping infant and was escorted to one of the squad cars, where she was content to stay out of the way and wait for Suzy and Nick.

Suzy watched as the man who'd almost killed her disappeared into the ambulance. "Who *is* he?" she asked Nick. "I still don't know."

"His name is Frank Kellerman. According to the information we have, he was Senator Merris's top aide," he told her.

That was the only thing that Nick could answer. He knew the man's identity. That had been checked into and verified after he'd been brought into the police station.

As for the rest of the questions surrounding this investigation, they still resided in the realm of the unknown. That included who the aide was currently working for and exactly what, if anything, Kellerman had to do with the three murder victims the graduate students had discovered during their dig.

Had Kellerman killed the three men? Or, if he hadn't, did he know who had? And what did any of this have to do with Melinda Grayson's apparent kidnapping?

Juarez had filled him in on the video that the dean had tried to call him about. That, too, answered only one question—that her disappearance was due to a kidnapping. But it raised so many more questions in its wake. If the professor *was* the victim of a kidnapping, why hadn't there been a ransom demand made, the way there had when Suzy's sister and baby were kidnapped?

What sort of game were the kidnappers playing?

Suzy nodded toward the departing ambulance. "He was the one who'd been calling me." It was a statement, but there was a question wrapped up in it. "What did he want with those photographs that Peter took? The man Peter wanted to blackmail is dead."

There was more than one person in those photographs. Which meant that there could be more than one vulnerable target—or not, Nick thought.

"Either Kellerman wanted to blackmail someone—or eliminate the possibility of that person being blackmailed by getting rid of the evidence." He sighed, running his hand through his unruly hair. He was still having trouble getting his heart rate down to a respectable rhythm. "Right now, your guess is as good as mine," he confessed to her.

He wasn't exactly feeling triumphant as a police detective, but at the moment, that all took a backseat to what he *was* feeling good about—the fact that he had arrived just in time to save the woman he'd fallen in love with from becoming one of Kellerman's victims.

This last event, he realized, had helped him put his life back into perspective. He was a cop and he loved being a cop, but being one—even a good one—hadn't made him feel whole. Loving Suzy, being part of her life, *that* was what had finally made him whole again.

And, he'd almost lost it all practically at the very moment that he'd found it.

"That was a very brave thing you did, going out on your own like that, trying to rescue your son and your sister."

She was about to demur, denying his praise, but she didn't get the chance just yet because he continued talking.

"—and if you *ever* do anything like that again, put me through anything like that again, I'll have you locked up for your own good faster than I can say 'I love you, Suzy,' do I make myself clear?" he demanded.

He had a smile on his face, but she had a feeling that he was dead serious.

"You can't threaten me like that for trying to save—wait," she cried, coming to a verbal, skidding halt as her brain replayed Nick's last words in her head. "What?" she demanded, grabbing hold of Nick's shirt to anchor him in place in case he had any plans on walking away from her without answering her question. "What did you just say to me?"

His expression never changed. "That I'd have you locked up—"

"No, no, not that part," she said impatiently, waving away his words. "The other part."

"You mean about loving you?" he asked innocently.

"Yes!" Suzy practically shouted the word at him. "That part."

He continued looking at her innocently. "What about it?"

"Do you?" she cried incredulously. Then, just to make it completely clear, she added, "Do you love me?"

This was a potentially fragile limb he was climbing out on and he knew it, especially since Suzy hadn't said anything even remotely in kind to him. But nothing ventured, nothing gained and he was growing extremely tired of spending his time gaining nothing.

"I wouldn't have said it if I didn't," he answered her simply. Then, because he didn't want her to feel obligated to reciprocate—he only wanted to hear her say it if she did so from the heart—he switched to a lighter tone and said, "Seems to me that you're going to need someone to keep an eye on you for a while, just to make sure that everything's all right." His smile was from the heart—and intended for hers. "I can't think of an assignment I'd welcome more."

She wasn't certain if Nick was teasing her—or on the level in this case. "So you don't think Andy and I are out of danger?" she asked uneasily.

"I'm not sure anyone is until all the pieces are put together and we find out exactly who killed your husband and just who's behind all the killings. Not to mention what this has to do with Professor Grayson's kidnapping, or who ordered Kellerman to take Lori and Andy."

"So you don't think Kellerman was acting on his own?" she asked. That would have at least made things a lot simpler for her. Because, if that were true, with Kellerman out of the picture, she could breathe more easily.

"Kellerman doesn't strike me as the type for independent thinking. He's more the lackey type, which means that he's trying to ingratiate himself to someone who he thinks is holding all the cards."

She thought of the senator, Kellerman's late boss. With him dead, that meant that Kellerman was now dancing to someone else's tune. "You mean 'the king is dead, long live the king'?"

Nick nodded. "Exactly."

She brushed her hand along her forehead. This was definitely making her brain ache. "My head hurts."

Suzy saw the look of concern that flashed through Nick's eyes. She hadn't meant to make him think something was wrong, but on the other hand, she found it comforting that someone cared about her, about her welfare and even how she physically felt. It had been a long, long time since someone—other than her sister—had.

"It's just a headache," she told him, waving it away. To prove that she was really all right, she said, "I guess you have to take my official statement now, right?"

Rather than leave now that everyone else was gone from the premises, Nick paused for a moment longer and brushed her hair away from her face. He laced his other hand through hers.

She thought to herself that she had never felt such a gentle, loving touch before.

"Tomorrow," Nick told her. "There's time enough for that tomorrow."

Suzy took in a long, shaky breath, then gave him her bravest smile. "I'd like to get it over with today if you don't mind." She knew that Lori would want to put the entire ordeal behind her as quickly as possible, too. He could take both their statements.

He nodded. At this point, he wasn't about to try to talk her out of anything. "Whatever you want."

She liked the sound of that.

The whole thing took longer than he'd expected.

When it was over, Nick took all of them home, acutely aware of the bullet they had all dodged today—literally.

Once at her house, which he insisted on thoroughly checking out just in case, he helped Suzy feed her son and get the infant ready for bed. Lori had murmured something about going to her apartment, but it was obvious that she would have felt more at ease spending the night with someone.

Suzy was quick to sense that. "You can stay here as long as you want, Lori. I owe you more than I can ever repay for what you went through. For what it's worth, my home is your home—you know that."

"Thanks," Lori said sincerely. "But it's not your fault there was a psycho on the loose." And then she smiled at her sister and Nick. "Now, if you don't mind, I really need to soak in the tub for a long time—maybe even a week," she speculated glibly. "So I'll just say good night now."

"Good night," Suzy called after her. "And thanks again!"

Lori raised her hand over her head, wiggling her fingers to show she'd heard but continued to make her way up the stairs.

"You know I'm not leaving tonight," Nick said to Suzy the moment her sister was out of sight.

"I was counting on it," Suzy told him as she laced her arms around his neck. "As a matter for fact, I'm not sure if I'm ever letting you go again."

"Works for me." He smiled into her eyes, then made her a solemn pledge. "I'll keep you safe, Suzy, you and Andy and your sister," he added, knowing what her family meant to her. What they had begun to mean to him. "I swear, I'll keep you safe."

"Busy," Suzy countered, brushing her lips against his as she said it. "I was hoping you'd keep me busy. I do love you, Detective Jeffries." She punctuated her statement by kissing him between every word she uttered.

She was doing it again, he thought, his pulse accelerating. She was making him crazy. Making him realize that for once in his life—and once was all it took—he'd lucked out. This time, he *knew* he'd found the right woman for him.

"That, too," he murmured agreeably just before they both lost themselves inside the fire that had just been ignited between them.

* * * * *

Don't miss the next story in our
VENGEANCE IN TEXAS *series,*
A RANCHER'S DEADLY AFFAIR
by Jennifer Morey,
available February 2012 from
Harlequin Romantic Suspense.

COMING NEXT MONTH FROM
HARLEQUIN® ROMANTIC SUSPENSE

Available January 22, 2013

#1739 BEYOND VALOR • *Black Jaguar Squadron*
by Lindsay McKenna

Though these two soldiers face death day after day, their greatest risk is taking a chance on each other.

#1740 A RANCHER'S DANGEROUS AFFAIR
Vengeance in Texas • by Jennifer Morey

Eliza's husband has been murdered, and she's in love with his brother. As guilt and love go to battle, Brandon may be the only one who can save her.

#1741 SOLDIER UNDER SIEGE • *The Hunted*
by Elle Kennedy

Special Forces soldier Tate doesn't trust anyone...especially the gorgeous woman who shows up on his doorstep asking him to kill a man.

#1742 THE LIEUTENANT BY HER SIDE
by Jean Thomas

Clare Fuller is forced to steal a mysterious amulet from army ranger Mark Griggs, but falling in love with him isn't in the plan. Nor is the danger that stalks them.

YOU CAN FIND MORE INFORMATION ON UPCOMING HARLEQUIN® TITLES, FREE EXCERPTS AND MORE AT WWW.HARLEQUIN.COM.

HRSCNM0113

REQUEST YOUR FREE BOOKS!
2 FREE NOVELS PLUS 2 FREE GIFTS!

H HARLEQUIN®

ROMANTIC suspense

Sparked by danger, fueled by passion

YES! Please send me 2 FREE Harlequin® Romantic Suspense novels and my 2 FREE gifts (gifts are worth about $10). After receiving them, if I don't wish to receive any more books, I can return the shipping statement marked "cancel." If I don't cancel, I will receive 4 brand-new novels every month and be billed just $4.49 per book in the U.S. or $5.24 per book in Canada. That's a savings of at least 14% off the cover price! It's quite a bargain! Shipping and handling is just 50¢ per book in the U.S. and 75¢ per book in Canada.* I understand that accepting the 2 free books and gifts places me under no obligation to buy anything. I can always return a shipment and cancel at any time. Even if I never buy another book, the two free books and gifts are mine to keep forever.

240/340 HDN FVS7

Name	(PLEASE PRINT)
Address	Apt. #
City	State/Prov.	Zip/Postal Code

Signature (if under 18, a parent or guardian must sign)

Mail to the **Harlequin® Reader Service:**
IN U.S.A.: P.O. Box 1867, Buffalo, NY 14240-1867
IN CANADA: P.O. Box 609, Fort Erie, Ontario L2A 5X3

Want to try two free books from another line?
Call 1-800-873-8635 or visit www.ReaderService.com.

* Terms and prices subject to change without notice. Prices do not include applicable taxes. Sales tax applicable in N.Y. Canadian residents will be charged applicable taxes. Offer not valid in Quebec. This offer is limited to one order per household. Not valid for current subscribers to Harlequin Romantic Suspense books. All orders subject to credit approval. Credit or debit balances in a customer's account(s) may be offset by any other outstanding balance owed by or to the customer. Please allow 4 to 6 weeks for delivery. Offer available while quantities last.

Your Privacy—The Harlequin® Reader Service is committed to protecting your privacy. Our Privacy Policy is available online at www.ReaderService.com or upon request from the Harlequin Reader Service.

We make a portion of our mailing list available to reputable third parties that offer products we believe may interest you. If you prefer that we not exchange your name with third parties, or if you wish to clarify or modify your communication preferences, please visit us at www.ReaderService.com/consumerschoice or write to us at Harlequin Reader Service Preference Service, P.O. Box 9062, Buffalo, NY 14269. Include your complete name and address.

SPECIAL EXCERPT FROM
HARLEQUIN® ROMANTIC SUSPENSE™

RS

Harlequin Romantic Suspense presents the first book in The Hunted, an edgy new miniseries from up-and-coming author Elle Kennedy

Living in hiding, Special Forces soldier Tate doesn't trust anyone…especially the gorgeous woman who shows up on his doorstep with a deadly proposition. But if he wants revenge on the man who destroyed his life, Tate has no choice but to join forces with Eva Dolce—and hope that he can keep his hands off her in the process….

Read on for an excerpt from

SOLDIER UNDER SIEGE

Available February 2013 from Harlequin Romantic Suspense

"How *did* you find me, Eva? I'm not exactly listed in any phone books."

She rested her suddenly shaky hands on her knees. "Someone told me you might be able to help me, so I decided to track you down. I'm…well, let's just say I'm very skilled when it comes to computers."

His jaw tensed.

"You're good, too," she added with grudging appreciation. "You left so many false trails it made me dizzy. But you slipped up in Costa Rica, and it led me here."

Tate let out a soft whistle. "I'm impressed. Very impressed, actually." He made a tsking sound. "You went to a lot of trouble to find me. Maybe it's time you tell me why."

"I told you—I need your help."

He raised one large hand and rubbed the razor-sharp stubble coating his strong chin.

A tiny thrill shot through her as she watched the oddly seductive gesture and imagined how it would feel to have those calloused fingers stroking her own skin, but that thrill promptly fizzled when she realized her thoughts had drifted off course again. What was it about this man that made her so darn aware of his masculinity?

She shook her head, hoping to clear her foggy brain, and met Tate's expectant expression. "Your help," she repeated.

"Oh really?" he drawled. "My help to do what?"

God, could she do this? How did one even begin to approach something like—

"For Chrissake, sweetheart, spit it out. I don't have all night."

She swallowed. Twice.

He started to push back his chair. "Screw it. I don't have time for—"

"I want you to kill Hector Cruz," she blurted out.

Will Eva's secret be the ultimate unraveling of their fragile trust? Or will an overwhelming desire do them both in? Find out what happens next in SOLDIER UNDER SIEGE

Available February 2013 only from Harlequin Romantic Suspense wherever books are sold.

Copyright © 2013 by Leeanne Kenedy

If thrilling romances and heart-racing action is what you're after, then check out Harlequin Romantic Suspense!

R S

NEW LOOK COMING DEC 18!

Featuring bold women, unforgettable men and the life-and-death situations that bring them together, these stories deliver!

ROMANTIC suspense

Four new stories available every month wherever books and ebooks are sold.

www.Harlequin.com

HRSPOST

Rediscover the Harlequin series section starting December 18!

NEW LOOK

·······

ON SALE DECEMBER 18

LONGER BOOK, NEW LOOK

·······

ON SALE DECEMBER 18

LONGER BOOK, NEW LOOK

·······

ON SALE DECEMBER 18

LONGER BOOK, NEW LOOK

·······

ON SALE DECEMBER 18

NEW SERIES HARLEQUIN KISS™!

·················

ON SALE JANUARY 22

www.Harlequin.com

HNEWS1212

HARLEQUIN®

NOCTURNE

Discover

THE KEEPERS: L.A.,

a dark and epic new paranormal quartet
led by *New York Times* bestselling author

HEATHER GRAHAM

New Keeper Rhiannon Gryffald has her peacekeeping
duties cut out for her. Because in Hollywood, it's hard
to tell the actors from the werewolves, bloodsuckers and
shape-shifters. When Rhiannon hears about a string of
murders that bear all the hallmarks of a vampire serial
killer, she must unite forces with sexy undercover
Elven agent Brodie to uncover a plot that may forever
alter the face of human-paranormal relations....

KEEPER OF THE NIGHT

by **Heather Graham,**
coming **December 18, 2012.**

And look for

Keeper of the Moon by Harley Jane Kozack—
Available March 5, 2013
Keeper of the Shadows by Alexandra Sokoloff—
Available May 7, 2013
Keeper of the Dawn by Heather Graham—
Available July 1, 2013

www.Harlequin.com

HN0113HGST

NOCTURNE

They never expected to fall for each other…

She's a committed sergeant in a top secret military unit.
He's a reluctant recruit—and a shape-shifter. But sparks fly
when Kristine and Quinn masquerade as honeymooners on a
beautiful island in search of Quinn's missing brother and his
new bride. Can the unlikely pair set aside their differences
in order to catch a killer bent on destroying Alpha Force?

FIND OUT IN

UNDERCOVER WOLF,

**a sexy, adrenaline-fueled new tale in the
Alpha Force miniseries from**

LINDA O. JOHNSTON

**Available February 5, 2013,
from Harlequin® Nocturne™.**

www.Harlequin.com

HN88564